LACKBIRD

HARPER TEEN
An Imprint of HarperCollinsPublishers

BLACKBIRD

ANNA CAREY

For Kev

HarperTeen is an imprint of HarperCollins Publishers.

Blackbird

Produced by Alloy Entertainment
1700 Broadway, New York, NY 10019
www.alloyentertainment.com

Library of Congress Cataloging-in-Publication Data
Carey, Anna.
  Blackbird / Anna Carey.
    pages cm
  Summary: "A teenage girl wakes up on the Los Angeles subway tracks with no
memory of who she is or how she got there. One thing she does know is that people
are trying to kill her, and she must race to uncover her past and outwit her hunters
before it's too late"— Provided by publisher.
  ISBN 978-0-06-229973-4 (hardback) — ISBN 978-0-06-236240-7 (int'l ed.)
  [1. Amnesia—Fiction. 2. Identity—Fiction. 3. Adventure and adventurers—Fiction.
4. Murder—Fiction. 5. Mystery and detective stories.] I. Title.
PZ7.C21Bl 2014   2014005806
[Fic]—dc23   CIP
                                                                                   AC

14 15 16 17 18   CG/RRDH   10 9 8 7 6 5 4 3 2 1
❖
First Edition

October 17, 2014

The dead body of a young woman was discovered by NYPD officers in Coney Island early Sunday morning. The woman had been shot to death. Her right hand was severed at the wrist and has not been found.

Police seek to identify the deceased woman. She is Caucasian and between eighteen and twenty-two years old.

CHAPTER ONE

THE TRAIN HOLDS the heat of the sun, even an hour after it has sunk beneath the pavement, pushing its way below the sprawling city. At the Vermont/Sunset Station, a Chinese woman with a severe black bob leans over the platform's edge, trying to gauge how far away the train is. A group of high school kids stands under a poster for some TV show, sharing iPod buds and discussing a boy called Kool-Aid. He is throwing a party this weekend in Echo Park while his parents move his older sister to one of the UCs.

You don't hear the kids laughing. They don't see you there, lying at the end of the tracks, where the tunnel disappears into darkness. It is the vibration that finally wakes you, your eyes fluttering open, the curved ceiling coming into view above. There's a heavy throbbing at your temples. The tracks are on either side of your shoulders, your spine pressed into the recess of the floor, where candy wrappers and worn newspapers have sat for months.

The horn wails. A sliver of light appears on the wall, casting out over the tile as the train pushes closer. You raise your head, bringing your chin to your chest, but your whole body is heavy. The feeling in your legs hasn't returned yet, and it's hard to turn your hips, hard to move at all, though you struggle, trying to pull yourself into the narrow space beneath the platform. When you fall back, exhausted, you spot the train at the tunnel's edge. It covers you in a sudden light.

The conductor has seen you. The sound the train makes changes—the brakes are a higher pitch now, more severe. It's too late. It is coming at you too fast. You only have one choice. You lie back, crossing your arms over your chest.

Three, two, one. At first it is all sound, the grinding of the wheels in the metal track, the rush of air as the train barrels forward. Its hot breath musses your hair. You stare into the train's dark underbelly, metal and pipe and wire. As the train finally slows, stopping in the station, it takes you a few seconds to process it: You are still lying there, just inches below the train. You're still alive.

On the platform above, the woman with the black bob can't believe what she has seen. Now, as the conductor steps from the front car, her face is cut by tears. "There's a girl down there. Didn't you see—there's a girl!" she yells.

The conductor is only thinking: *She was lying down, she couldn't move, why was she lying down?* This is the fourth one he has seen in twenty-six years, but the three before were different. They weren't like her. Some stand, some throw themselves. Others have fallen and tried to pull themselves back onto the platform. But she was just lying there. So specifically positioned, arms crossed over her chest, shoulders just inside the tracks. *It's too strange,* he thinks. *Like someone left her there.*

From under the train, you can hear the woman yell. Her voice breaks, and a man tries to comfort her. Shadows move in the space between the train car and the platform ledge. A bell rings and people file off, footsteps mixing with questions.

"I'm okay," you call out. Your voice surprises you. It is small and raspy, like a child's.

On the platform, a man repeats your words. "She's okay!" He has pushed his way to the front of the crowd, kneeling just a few feet above.

The conductor calls, "Are you hurt?"

On first glance it looks like oil, the way it trickles down the side of your forearm and catches in your shirt. The blood is that dark, almost black. But you don't feel any pain, just a burning sensation, as if you're standing too close to a radiator.

"I'm okay," you repeat. The gash can't be more than four inches long. It doesn't look that deep.

The conductor debates with a colleague about whether or not to pull the train back out. They radio in to the headquarters to consult, while the woman with the blunt bob calls 911, giving a frantic account of the ordeal. They are sending help.

It feels like you are there forever. You can't look at the bottom of the train without wanting to scream. Instead you close your eyes, trying to draw your arms into yourself, making the space bigger so you don't feel so trapped. It's automatic, the way you slow your breaths, counting them out, letting just a thin stream of air move through your parted lips.

Finally there's an ambulance wail, the sound of medics assembling on the platform above. Then they yell directions, telling you where to put your arms, your legs, as if you'd dare move. The train finally pulls out. You are watching the bottom of the subway cars pass, until there is nothing above you but air. The feeling in your legs has returned. You're able to sit up, but two men in uniform jump from the platform ledge with a board, lifting you onto it. It's only then that you notice the black backpack by your feet.

"What happened? How'd you get there?" one of the medics asks as they pull you up toward the platform.

You glance down at your outfit, staring at a body that feels completely unfamiliar to you. The front of your T-shirt is wet with blood. You're wearing new jeans and new shoes. The laces are a stiff, electric white.

"I don't know," you say, unable to place the time or day, unable to conjure even one detail of your life. There is only this moment, nothing more.

"You don't remember? What's your name?" The other medic is a short, stocky man with tattoos climbing up his right arm. The sight of two skulls, roses twisting around them, triggers something in you. Sadness? Grief?

They lift the board onto the platform, one pulling things from his bag. "It's okay; I'm okay," you repeat, looking at the escalator a few feet away. It's the only exit.

One of the medics shines a light in your eyes, then your mouth. You push yourself to sit, wriggling off the board and onto the cement floor. You pull your bag closer. "I don't need help," you say. "I'm fine."

"You're not fine," the medic presses. "What's your name?"

A crowd has formed around you. You search your mind but it feels like an empty room, with no couch cushions to turn over, no cabinets or drawers to rifle through. Instead you reach for the knapsack's zipper, pretending you know what is inside.

Foil pouches of water and food, a blanket, an extra T-shirt, a red pocketknife, and a pile of items too buried to reach. Your hands move to the tiny black notepad on top, a pen tucked in its front cover. A quarter is taped to the first page.

Beneath it reads: *Do not contact the police. When you are alone, call 818-555-1748.*

You stand, slipping around the two stunned medics, past the crowd and into the stifling station. "You can't just leave," the medic says. "Someone grab her; she's not thinking straight."

You're still dizzy as you climb the escalator, the crowd falling back behind you. You push through the turnstile. The stairs go up and up, the steps endless. As you run a few people in the crowd call out to you, one trailing behind, demanding you sit and rest.

"Don't go; wait. Don't go."

There's no time. When you get to the top of the station stairs a police car is already turning the corner, pulling up along the curb. You give the intersection a quick glance: The streets are labeled SUNSET and VERMONT. There are office buildings, sub shops, and smoothie places. Which direction should you go?

You turn, seeing the medic with the tattoos. He is at the police officer's elbow, speaking to him in a low voice. The officer takes only a few steps toward you, not quite walking, not quite running, when you make the decision. You hold the straps of the knapsack and set off into a sprint.

CHAPTER TWO

THERE IS ONLY the sound of your breaths, the quiet thudding of your sneakers rolling off the sidewalk. Each step is good and easy, your back straight as if you're being pulled from above. You cut through someone's front yard and hop a low wood fence. Slowly, block after block, the neighborhood twists into the dry hills, a view peeking out beyond the trees.

Up ahead there's a house. Clay roof, high hedges. The half-moon window in the front is dark. You push through the gate and into the yard, spotting a flower bush several feet wide. You crawl underneath it, letting your stomach press against the cool earth, a momentary relief from the heat.

You stay there as a police car rolls past, pausing several times as it winds back down the street. When you turn on your side, you notice the mark inside your right wrist. It's still sore, the tattoo covered in a thin scab. A bird silhouetted inside a box. Letters and numbers are printed just below: *FNV02198.*

What does it mean? Why were you just lying on the subway tracks? Why can't you remember how you ended up there, how you got to that station, this city? You look down at your clothes, feeling like you're in costume. The jeans don't fit, the T-shirt is baggy in the wrong places, and your laces aren't tied tight enough. You can't shake the sickening feeling that you didn't dress yourself.

A dog barks. Somewhere two little girls giggle, their voices rising and falling as they swing higher on a creaky swing set. Cars pass on the street below. You sit there, listening to each sound as if it's a clue. *Think,* you tell yourself. *Remember.* But there is nothing there. No words, no thoughts. No memories of anything that came before.

When the sky turns from pink to black you crawl onto the lawn and dump the contents of the pack on the scorched grass, sorting them quickly in a straight line. There are a few plastic zip ties. There's a map with a star marked in black pen. Foil bags, the T-shirt, the notepad and pocketknife, the blanket, and a red vial of mace.

You dig into the last pockets of the bag, double-checking the lining to make sure there's nothing hidden inside. There's a wad of money in the knapsack's front. You thumb through it, your hands unsteady. It's one thousand dollars.

You open the notepad to a fresh page, smooth down the paper, and write:

Things I know are true:
- I am in Los Angeles
- I woke up on the train tracks at the Vermont/Sunset Station
- I am a girl
- I have long black hair
- I have a bird tattoo on the inside of my right wrist (FNV021987)
- I am a runner

CHAPTER THREE

THE NEXT MORNING, you leave through a break in the back fence. After ten minutes winding down and around the narrow roads, the neighborhood turns to flat streets, sun-scorched front lawns, and the occasional store. A main strip reveals a supermarket with a pay phone outside. You pull the notepad from your pack and flip to the first page, prying off the quarter.

It falls through the slot but there's no dial tone. You set the handset down and scan the street, hoping there's another pay phone within a block or two. But all you see is the police cruiser pulling into the far entrance. You're still close to the subway station, and you wonder if they're looking for you. You don't want to risk it. You head inside, holding your arm to the front of your shirt to hide the bloodstain.

The electric doors slide back in greeting. The first thing you notice is the air, cold and damp and smelling of mint.

To your left, beyond a cluster of tables, is a bathroom door. You keep your head down as you move toward it, trying to avoid attention.

The door swings open, the edge of it catching your arm. A boy steps forward, his shoulder knocking you hard in the nose. You stumble and he grabs you, his hands cupping your elbows as he pulls you to him, steadying you.

Behind him, another kid slips out of the bathroom, tucking something into his pocket. Within a few seconds he's gone.

Your nose is throbbing from where he knocked into you, the pain so intense your eyes squeeze shut. He doesn't let go of you. He moves your right hand away from your stomach, the gesture so tender you don't resist. He studies the stain on your shirt and the gash in your forearm, which has dried a deep cherry black.

"You're hurt," he says.

His brown hair is a mess, the curls hiding the tops of his ears. The sun has turned his skin tan and freckly. He watches you, his gray eyes scanning your face like he's reading a book.

"I just need to wash up, that's all." You pull your arm away and slip inside the bathroom.

You can't relax until the door clicks shut behind you, the lock turned in place. When you look in the mirror you see what he sees. The dirt caked in your hairline, the bits of dried leaves caught there. The stain on your shirt is a putrid brown. You study your reflection for the first time. Your large, deep-set eyes are so dark they're almost black. You have high cheekbones and a small, heart-shaped mouth. Your features are unfamiliar to you, the face of a girl you've never seen before.

You turn to the side, and that's when you notice the scar stretching from under your right ear to the nape of your neck, the skin puckered and red. You trace your fingers to where it disappears behind the collar of your shirt. It's still tender in places, the wound twisting in a strange, uneven line. You turn away, not wanting to think about how or when you got it. It's not from the train, you know that. When did it happen? How?

It takes a few minutes to scrub the dirt from under your fingernails, to change into the fresh T-shirt and pick bits of leaves from your hair. When you're done you look better, passable even. You pull your hair over your shoulder so it covers the scar.

Outside, you scan the supermarket for the boy. Part of you hopes he's gone, but part of you is glad when he's there, just a few feet away, walking through the greeting-card section. He turns when the door falls closed, a small smile forming on his lips. You look around, wondering if the cop came inside.

You take a hard left down the first aisle. No one's there.

You pull a water bottle from the shelf, unscrewing the cap. You've drank half the bottle when you notice the boy beside you. His eyes move from the water, back to you, then to the empty space on the shelf.

"You look a lot better."

"Like I said, I just needed to clean up."

You step away from him, moving farther down the aisle, but he trails a few feet behind. He looks at your arm, the toilet paper pressed to the wound, now speckled red.

"What happened? You okay?"

"It looks worse than it is. I'm fine, really."

He doesn't turn away. "It looked pretty bad."

"My arm is the least of my problems. . . ."

You scan the front of the store, looking again for the cop. You've lost sight of him. The other boy from the bathroom is gone. "What did you sell him?" you ask.

"What do you mean?"

"In the bathroom . . . you sold that kid something. Pot? Pills? What?"

The boy passes a basket between his hands, two sad apples rolling around beside a six-pack of Coke. "You don't know that."

"I do." It was obvious, the way he held whatever was in his pocket, as if you might see it or take it away. "I just saw a cop outside. You should at least be smart about it."

"What do you know about that?" The boy inches closer,

looking at you with new interest. There's something friend-lier in him now, as if he underestimated you.

"Mind if I use your phone a second?" You nod to his front pocket, the rectangle pressing against the cloth.

"Yeah, I guess." He passes it to you. "You don't have one?"

"If I had one do you think I'd be asking?"

You take a few steps from him before pulling the notepad from your bag, opening it to the page with the number. The nervousness hits as you wait, listening to the silence before the first ring. You can't help but hate the person on the other line, whoever they are, for knowing more about your life than you do.

Three rings, then a man's voice. "I was wondering if you'd call."

The boy is less than ten feet away, pretending to look at some boxes of cereal. You lower your voice when you speak. "Who is this?"

"Just meet me at my office. It's the building marked on that map. Come alone."

You're trying to read into his words, to decipher some meaning beyond what's said, but then he hangs up and there is only the time. Eighteen seconds and he's gone.

The boy is listening, so you talk into nothingness, offer-ing good-byes and thanks. Scrolling through the phone, you move quickly to the call history to delete the number. *Mom, Mom, Mom,* reads the list below it. As you hand the phone back the boy narrows his eyes. "What are you laughing at?"

"Nothing," you say, and you are already taking a step back. "Thanks for that. I have to run."

But when you turn, the police officer is at the end of the aisle. He's in profile, his fingers grazing a rack of chips. He glances up, noticing you notice him.

You turn back to the boy. "Unless . . . Can you give me a ride somewhere?"

He sets the basket on the floor, the Coke now buried under two boxes of Cap'n Crunch. "Where do you need to go?"

"Downtown."

He nods toward the exit, urging you off. You walk beside him, your shoulders nearly touching, and it takes all you have not to turn around, not to look one last time at the officer at the back of the store. When you get to the register the boy empties the basket onto the conveyor belt, the apples rolling in opposite directions.

"I'm Ben, by the way."

The mention of his name makes you nervous, and you wonder why you didn't think of it before. *People* and *Us Weekly* are crammed into a rack in front of you, a magazine called *Sunset* right beside them.

"I'm Sunny," you lie. It seems as good a name as any. It seems real.

Then you glance back one last time, just to be certain the officer isn't there.

CHAPTER FOUR

THE JEEP SPEEDS past dusty buildings and empty parking lots, an alley with ripped tarp tents. You watch the world outside pass, certain you have done something wrong. Stolen something, run away from somewhere—school? Home? There's no other reason why you'd be warned not to contact the police, why you'd be waiting for a stranger to tell you who you are. Why were you so intent to get away, why was your instinct to run? Why can't you remember anything from before?

Just the thought of it makes you wince. You were someone before this. And if there is a line between good and bad, you were probably on the wrong side of it. You were the one escaping, the one running, the one trying not to get caught. The scar on your neck might be something you deserved.

"I don't know what you're thinking," Ben says, "but it's not that bad. I just do it for extra cash."

"I wasn't thinking about that," you say.

"I don't even use the stuff," Ben goes on. "I quit a while ago."

"Seriously . . ." you say, looking out the window as block after block flies past. "I'm not going to tell anyone. Don't worry."

Ben makes a left turn on Broadway, nearly sideswiping a Fiat parked at the corner. "My history teacher says it's senioritis. That none of us care. We're all just waiting to graduate, so we're doing stupid things. He wasn't talking about drugs; it was more . . . everything. I'm only in class seventy percent of the time."

"Where are you the other thirty?"

"Hanging out at home."

"Don't your parents care?"

"My mom's not around much."

"Why?"

"She's been sick." Ben slows the car. He scans the few blocks up ahead, close to where you told him you were going. In that pause he says everything: *Leave it alone, no more questions, just something I told you and I'm hoping you'll ignore.*

"Come on, you have to at least tell me where I'm taking you."

"I'm going here." You point to the curb half a block up. You tried to keep the conversation neutral during the twenty-minute ride, making fun of the Red Bull cans strewn about the car floor, listening to Ben describe Marshall High School, the public school he's been going to for the last few years, since he got kicked out of a private. But every now and then Ben asked about your arm or what happened this morning, why your jeans were ripped. You only pulled the map out once and you tried not to let him see, but he kept glancing over, his eyes narrowing at the star scribbled in pen.

Ben pulls up next to a metal fence. Across an empty lot, two men sit under a lean-to, sharing a cigarette. There are gang tags on the brick wall. "You want me to drop you off here?"

"This is perfect."

"Perfect?" When Ben says it, his voice rises, the word giving way to laughter. The building on the map is five blocks away, but you won't risk having him bring you there.

The Jeep has just pulled to a stop when you open the door, stepping down onto the sidewalk. Ben riffles through his glove compartment, scavenges the center console and floor. When he finds a pen he scribbles on the back of a crumpled receipt, then hands it to you. It's a phone number.

"In case of emergency?" you ask.

"In case it's not perfect. Or if you need anything. Whatever."

You fold the receipt into a square and tuck it in the front pocket of your jeans. "Thanks for the ride."

The door is closed. The engine is still running, both his hands on the steering wheel as he looks at the buildings across the street, trying to figure out where it is you're headed. Two breaths. He gives you a half smile, then finally shifts the car into drive.

When he's gone you start past the empty lot, past a building labeled CLUB STARLIGHT, its awning faded to gray. The streets are practically deserted. You pass the Orpheum Theatre, the banner advertising some band you've never heard of. Then, within a few more steps, you see the curved entranceway jutting out over the sidewalk.

The lobby is empty. The doorman's post is abandoned, not even a guest book or pen left on top of the podium. You look into the far corner of the room, where a security camera is perched like a bird. You turn your head away, bringing your hand to your temple to block your profile, hoping the angle wasn't right, that it didn't catch you straight on.

A plastic directory on the wall lists the companies, but all of the names are unfamiliar. You scan through the numbers instead. Past finance companies and therapist offices you find GARNER CONSULTING, SUITE 909, 818-555-1748. It's the same number from your notebook.

You take the elevator to the ninth floor. When the doors open the hallway is empty, the carpet stitched with a strange arrow pattern that points you forward. Somewhere a loud copier is spitting out pages. You pause at the suite marked

909, listening to the quiet beyond the door. There are no footsteps, no voices, no shuffling of papers.

No one answers when you knock. You knock again, louder this time, but no one comes. You sit against the wall, your knapsack between your legs, when an idea comes. You draw the pocketknife from your backpack and flip it open, the blade catching the light. You wedge the blade between the lock and the doorframe, angling the tip so it puts pressure on the mechanism. After a few seconds of maneuvering, it pops, the door springing open.

You know you've done it a hundred times before. It was too easy, too quick, your hands so steady and sure. You return to the thoughts from the car: *You have done something wrong.*

The door opens and you half expect to see someone there, sitting behind the desk or in one of the chairs lining the wall. The room is empty, the computer screen dark. Magazines are fanned out on a kidney-shaped table. *The Economist, National Geographic, Time.*

The desk is covered with a blotter and a gold cup crammed with pens. There's a framed photo of two blond children sitting on a dock. Their feet splash in the water. You take a few steps beyond the sitting room, turning past a frosted-glass wall with GARNER CONSULTING written in metallic script. You turn the knob and an alarm begins to wail.

You cover your ears and look around. Cash is strewn

across the carpet. A safe sits in the corner, its door half open, the lock scuffed and broken. The desk chair has been turned on its side. The drawers are emptied over the floor, papers and folders everywhere.

You remind yourself that you haven't taken anything, haven't even touched the safe or the cash. You are here because you were told to come. Still, you think only of the security camera downstairs, the knife in your pocket, how easily you broke in.

Outside, in the hallway, several people have already emerged from their offices. A man in a three-piece suit stares at you over his wire glasses. "I don't know what happened," you say, looking at two women hovering beside him. One is on her phone. "I didn't do anything."

The man looks at your knapsack, then down the hall, where a few more workers huddle together. You wonder how long you have before they move toward the elevator or the stairs, blocking the exits. There are only seconds to decide: try to explain, or run.

You run.

CHAPTER FIVE

THE SALESGIRL IS watching a cartoon when you walk in, her eyes on the small flat-screen television in the corner of the room. Three dresses are slung over her arm. As she sorts through them she turns to you, studying your face.

"Can I help you?" she calls out.

"Just looking." You disappear down a side aisle.

She takes a few steps so she can see you. It must be your stained jeans, the dirty, sweat-soaked T-shirt. You look like the type of person who would shoplift, and you can't help but feel she's not that far off. You are already gauging how easy it would be to pull a bunch of shirts from the rack, slip two or three into your bag when she's not looking, and just leave. You start down another aisle and she finally turns away.

You spent nearly twelve hours across the street from the office building, crouching in the back of a parking garage, hidden behind a pickup truck. You watched the police come and go, the building empty out as the sky went black. It was nearly two in the morning when you found a cab, the driver off duty, parked and sleeping around the corner, directing him to take you back north.

You spent the night beneath a playground. Sand is still everywhere—embedded in your socks, gathered in the pockets of your pants, hidden behind your ears. You still wonder if you should call the police. You can't explain yourself to them. Ever since you left you've been thinking about your hand on the doorknob, the knife pushing against the lock to break it open.

You move through the rack, picking up a black T-shirt with a faint logo on it. A snake is coiled around a rose. There's a tight tank top, some jean shorts, their pockets visible through the ripped fronts. It's easy finding the things you like. You're cradling them in your arms when you notice the alternative—plain cotton shirts and khaki shorts, a belt with a metal sunflower for the clasp. You ditch the armful and go for the more basic things, as if constructing a costume.

The phone on the counter rings. The clerk picks it up, says hello to some guy named Cosmo. She tells him about an audition as she begins ringing you up.

"No, it's for the part of the acupuncturist," the girl says, the phone pinned to her shoulder. She pulls a T-shirt across the glass counter, her gaze dropping again to your stained pants.

On the TV behind her, the commercials end and the morning news begins. The anchor looks plastic, with a straight, shiny nose and brows sewn up toward his forehead. He introduces a segment about a bear on the loose in Agoura Hills. Cut to another story about school budgets. The sales-clerk fumbles with one of the shirt tags. She gestures to a rack as if to say: *I have to get a price.*

She is epically slow, pausing every few moments to talk on the phone, her hand darting in and out of the rack. You lean both elbows on the counter, careful to keep your right arm under your left, the wound out of sight. You can feel the raised skin inside your wrist, where the tattoo is. It's still tender to the touch. FNV02198. It's possible it's your birthday, that February 1, 1998, would put you at sixteen years old, turning seventeen in a few months. It could be your initials. Farrah Natasha Valente, Faith Neely Vargas . . . the guesses are comforting.

By the time they show the picture you are only half there. You recognize the lobby first, the empty podium and the square windows above the entranceway. "Police are look-ing for information regarding a robbery in downtown Los Angeles." There's the shot of you looking into the security camera. Another from outside the office suite. You have the knife wedged in the door, in the process of breaking open the lock. "Police say the thief made off with over ten thousand dollars. If you have any information regarding this robbery please contact Crime Stoppers."

The girl returns, glancing at the television, then at you, her eyes lingering for a moment on your hair, then your shirt. You turn to the shelf behind you, grabbing a pair of vintage glasses, covering them with two blouses you swipe from another rack. When she glances away you tuck the glasses in your back pocket and add the shirts to the pile. She looks again at the television but the news program has gone to commercial.

As you pass the sales clerk a fifty you try to keep your hand steady. It was stupid of you to come back here, only blocks away from the subway station. You returned last night because it's the only place you know, but it can't be long before someone recognizes you. For the first time since you awoke you feel your throat tighten, your eyes so wet you have to turn away, afraid the girl might see.

When she hands you the bag you keep your gaze on the floor. She is still on the phone as you leave, pushing into the sickening heat, the chimes jangling overhead.

———

The motel room is quiet. The window faces a brick wall. You stand there, staring at your new reflection in the mirror behind the door.

You showered, combed your hair out, toweled off the

dirt and grime. Your blunt-cut bangs sit right above your eyebrows. The lenses in your glasses are thin and plastic, the frames a clear Lucite. The long-sleeve shirt you bought has purple flowers on the collar and sleeves. It's something a woman in a nursing home might wear.

It's not you—not the light-wash jeans or the belt you pulled from the rack. Not even the plastic watch. You know this, even if you don't know anything else. You are playing a character. Nondescript Girl. A little homely, a little prim. Even your reflection is unfamiliar.

In the distance, someone leans on a car horn. You try to lie down on the bed but it feels too soft, too strange, so you arrange the sheets and blankets on the carpet. You pull on a T-shirt and take off the glasses, stretching out beside the bed. Your back feels good against the floor and you close your eyes, imagining that if you stay like this for long enough the world outside might be different when you open them. You could wake up knowing who you are, the scar in the mirror at once familiar. You will wake up and know. . . . You might wake up and know. . . .

You lie there, listening to the sounds outside. You sling your arm over your face, covering your eyes with the crook of your elbow, blocking out the light. You shift, you curl to the side. Sleep still doesn't come.

You run through the list again, turning over the facts, sorting them out like tiny precious stones. You woke up on the subway tracks in Los Angeles. You were led to an office downtown that was set up to look as though you'd robbed it. You know how to open a door with a knife blade, and you've probably done it many times before.

Whoever drew you there didn't just want you to stay away from the police, they needed to be certain you couldn't go to them, no matter how desperate you were. They meant for you to get caught . . . but why?

You don't want to turn on the TV, afraid you might see the photo again. Instead you pick up the motel phone and dial the number from the notepad. The number of Garner Consulting. It rings and rings and rings. You hang up and try again, then again, but still no one answers.

When the silence becomes unbearable you open the nightstand drawers, going through them, looking for something to occupy your thoughts. They're all empty except for the top one, which contains a black leather book. The words *Holy Bible* are embossed in gold letters. You can't stop looking at the red ribbon that marks the page. You pick it up, running the thin strip of satin between your fingers. You flip to a page and the memory rushes in, the smell of incense coming back.

The sound surrounds you, that sad, hollow clank of your dress shoes against the marble floor.

It's all so clear. As you move up the aisle you don't dare look at the pews beside you. Instead your gaze remains on the coffin. It sits just in front of the altar, on a metal accordion-spring riser with wheels on the bottom. It's shrouded in a white linen sheet. As you pass you set your palm on top of it, imagining that your hand could sink right through, down through the wood and stuffing and fabric, until it was on top of his. It wasn't his body, his face, it was just an empty shell, as if the life had crawled out of him. How long had you knelt by the casket? Who had come and pulled you away? Then there was that sound—that shuddering, awful sound of the lid as the attendant closed it. A woman had hunched forward, face in hands. She hadn't been able to watch.

Don't look at them, *you think, stepping onto the altar. You grip either side of the podium, trying to steady yourself. The church is empty except for the cluster of people in the first row. You can already feel them watching you, their full eyes waiting. You glance at the pews in the back, a quick acknowledgment before staring down at the book.*

You play with the satin ribbon that marks the page. You take a long, thin breath. The last thing you hear is your voice, somewhere outside your body, the words practically a whisper.

"A reading from Ecclesiastes."

Then the motel room rises up around you. You are back, sitting on the edge of the bed, the sights and sounds of the memory gone. You drop the Bible back into the drawer and close it. Your face feels foreign and strange, and for a brief second you're so relieved to have remembered something you actually smile.

It's a passing moment, swept away by a sudden flood. *Someone has died, someone has died.* You don't know who he was or how it happened, but it feels as though some crucial organ has been cut out of you and life will be harder now, more perilous. You fold in on yourself, the tears hot in your eyes.

He's dead, you think, not knowing who, only that he mattered. *You loved him and he died.*

CHAPTER SIX

YOU PICK APART the donut. The slushy orange drink is too sweet. The DJ's voice on the radio rises and falls in endless, annoying cheer. As you sit at the table in the back of the diner, you only notice the high-pitched, cackling laugh of the cashier, the incessant buzzing of the lights overhead.

Beyond the glass window, cars speed down Vine Street. The heat is so intense you can see it, the air taking on an undulating, liquid quality. You riffle through the knapsack, finally locating the notepad. You write the events of yesterday, feeling better when you are doing something, anything. You try to remember the exact words the news anchor used to describe the robbery. You pull the receipts from your pocket, jotting down the totals from food and the thrift store. Even after paying for the motel room you still have over eight hundred dollars.

You turn the page, going back to the list from before. The memory is hazy. You can't recall the color of the woman's hair. Brown? Gray? You just remember her hands, the thin, papery skin, her fingers pressed to her temples as she covered her face. You can't say the color shirt she was wearing, you never looked at the paintings on the church's back wall. Instead you write the only things that were clear:

- I had a memory of a church
- Someone close to me died (a father, brother, uncle, grandfather?)
- I was reading at his funeral
- A woman (my mother?) also lost this person
- There were less than a dozen people there

Your pen rests on the paper, just below the last line, and you want there to be more. You want to write something definitive, but all you're left with is this sinking feeling, the grief covering you like a thin film.

You tuck the notepad away. As you reassemble the pack you're uneasy. Something feels strange . . . off. A man with a ratty gray beard stands at the register, trading a fistful of change for a single donut. A woman with a missing front tooth reads a magazine. You turn, scanning the yellow plastic booths behind you, and that's when you notice him.

He has thinning brown hair and tiny, marble-like eyes.

He watches you in an obvious, unashamed way, not even trying to pretend he's not. He wears a shirt and tie, the white fabric soaked under his armpits. You stare right back, everything in you tense, but he doesn't look away.

Your body feels weightless and cold. You leave the tray where it is, not bothering to clean up the trash scattered across the table. You grab your backpack and start toward the door, but in the few seconds it takes you to reach it he is already standing, dropping his wallet and keys in his back pockets.

You start down the stairs and out into the street, trusting the cars will stop when you cut across. A truck slows a half block up. The driver leans on the horn. All the lights are green and more cars speed toward you as you run, your skin covered in a quick sweat.

When you're finally across you wonder if you imagined it, if the danger was as real as it felt. You turn back just in time to see the man in the parking lot. He gets into a silver car. There's a dent in the side, the gash stretching from the back bumper to the front door. His fingers rest on the edge of the open window. You can't tell if he's recognized you from the news photos or he knows you from before. There's nothing about him that feels familiar. He's still watching you, his eyes in the rearview mirror as he pulls the car out.

You cut through a side street and disappear into a parking structure. The sign reads ARCLIGHT CINEMAS. An arrow directs you up an entrance ramp and you weave through parked cars, eventually coming out into an interior court-yard. Inside the lobby, lines snake from the cashier around to the café. You maneuver through the crowd, past an elderly man in an Oakland A's cap and a pack of overly made-up women. You push out the front of the building. A group of teenagers has just left the theater. There are ten of them, maybe more, and you keep close, trailing only a few steps behind.

As they start down a set of stairs you walk beside the group as if you've always been there. One boy has a skate-board tucked under his arm. He holds out an ID to his friend. "Maryland," he says. "It works as long as they don't scan it."

The girl has a bright purple streak in her hair. She turns the ID over, tilts it back and forth in the light. "You got this at that smoke shop on Hollywood and Western?"

You are shoulder to shoulder with them, walking along Sunset Boulevard, when you glance behind you. The man has pulled the car around. He stops at the intersection, his left blinker on, ready to circle the block. He's following you. You're certain of it.

You move closer to the group, positioning yourself on the inside so you're not as visible. The girls beside you are talking about a concert they went to and the black lipstick they picked up at CVS. It's strange to listen to them recall the tiny, ordinary details of their lives.

"Hey . . . do you guys know where I can get some Molly?" you say, waiting a few seconds to let it sink in.

A boy in front bursts out laughing. A few "oh, shits" echo through the group.

"Are you crazy?" The boy with the skateboard looks at your ill-fitting jeans and shirt, taking note of the dainty purple flowers on your collar. "You can't just walk up to people and ask them for drugs. What are you thinking?"

"I'm thinking I want some Molly." It's provocative, but it works—they close in around you. You have their attention.

"You could be a cop," a boy with braces says.

"I didn't know there were sixteen-year-old cops."

The girl with the purple streak in her hair laughs. "I guess there aren't, huh?"

You pause at the intersection, watching the sign across the street, the blinking red hand telling you *Don't walk, don't walk.* You keep your head down, but out of the corner of your eye you can see his car approaching. The man drives past, moving up Sunset. There is a decal on the trunk. ASK ME ABOUT REAL ESTATE. You look below, where the license plate should be, but it's gone.

He stops at the next corner and puts his blinker on, preparing to take a left down a side street. You're at the front of the group, watching him go, when your eyes meet his in the rearview mirror. As he turns the corner your legs are dead weight.

"Helloooo? Did you hear me?" the boy with the skate-board asks, nudging you to cross the street.

"Yeah, I'm listening." You move deeper inside the crowd as you cross, but it's hard to pretend you were paying atten-tion. You look over your shoulder, waiting for the car to reappear.

The boy drops his skateboard on the ground, pushes off and away. After a beat he pauses on the sidewalk just ahead of you. He holds up a hand, gesturing for the others to stay quiet. "You're not with the cops?"

"I told you. No."

He points over your shoulder. You turn, looking where he looks. The man is there. He's parked the car out of sight. He turns the corner, his steps fast as he approaches.

"So that guy's not with you?"

You push ahead of him, trying to steady your voice. "No, he's not."

"How long has he been there?" the boy asks.

"He followed me out of Winchell's." You squeeze past, knocking into the skateboard tucked under his arm. "I have to go. Please don't let him see me."

The boy steps between you and the man, blocking his view. You don't run, instead doubling your pace, trying not to draw too much attention as you move ahead. You're at the opposite corner when you hear the boy yell, "What are you doing, creep? Stop following her."

You turn, watching the girl with the purple streak grab his arm. The boy pushes his shoulder. The man shakes them off, jerks his fist back like he's going to hit them. He steps to the side, then slinks away. He's muttering something, but you can't hear what.

You're grateful for even that little bit of time. Their voices mix with the sounds of traffic, of cars picking up speed as the light turns green. There's a massive store just half a block ahead. You check behind you, watching a boy with a nose piercing yell at the man. Then you duck inside.

The place is cavernous. Records and CDs are crammed into bins, album covers plastered on every wall. A man in an Amoeba Music T-shirt stacks boxes on a metal cart. You slow your steps, pretending to be any other customer, but your pulse is so fast you can feel it in your fingers.

There's only one choice when you're inside. Go to a narrow back room or up the metal staircase to your right. The rest of the store is open space, row upon row of plastic shelving. You go straight to the back. Two store clerks are so busy restocking DVDs that they don't look up as you pass.

A rack of T-shirts runs along the far wall. There are hundreds of them. When you reach the corner, out of sight from most of the customers, you duck down. You part the wire hangers then sit back against the wall, pulling some of the shirts to cover you. A Nirvana sweatshirt has fallen by your feet and you use it to hide your sneakers.

You part the shirts just enough to see out. From where you sit you have a view of the first aisle and the space by the doorway. Two girls breeze past. One yanks a DVD from the rack and studies it, then puts it back.

The radio is playing a familiar song. You don't know the words but you recognize the melody, and that alone is comforting. You are bent over, your chin resting on your knees, arms hugging your legs, when he crosses into the back room. He circles around to the second aisle. You catch glimpses of his shirt, his shoulder, the side of his face. You quiet your breaths when he turns down the aisle.

For a moment he is only a few feet away. You can see him from the chest down. He pushes his hand deep into his pocket. He pauses there, so close his breaths are audible. You stay as still as you can as he withdraws a phone and begins dialing. Then he turns, scanning the room one last time before he leaves.

You rest your head on your knees, finally releasing your breath. You dig your fingernails into your palm until it hurts, angry you went into that diner right then. Angry you're here, in Los Angeles, still. It was only a matter of time before someone spotted you. The real question is who he is and why he cared enough to follow you.

Tourists swarm the back room. Five of them are in front of you, their orthopedic shoes just inches from your feet. They pull shirts from the rack, chatting about hiking to the Hollywood sign. An attendant helps a customer find *Breathless*. The song changes again and again.

When you're certain he's gone, you move, taking some of the shirts for yourself, shoving them into the bottom of your knapsack. You pull one over your head, double-checking there's no plastic tags or metal stickers on the inside. You leave as quickly as you came, sneaking out from under the rack. When you push through the doors, you're careful to keep your head down, trying to avoid the store's security cameras.

Outside, Sunset Boulevard is busy. Restaurants and bars empty into the street. Even when you're several blocks away, deep into a neighborhood, you are looking for him. He is every silver car, every figure approaching on the sidewalk. You cut through someone's backyard and start through the trees.

CHAPTER SEVEN

THE WOMAN IS waiting to hear her name. She is only waiting to hear her name. She is so tired of these dinners, these receptions, these people—all she wants is to receive her award. So when Silvia O'Connor, Bill's wife, leans over to her, mentioning something about the salad, she is truly annoyed. Silvia is whispering, "Oh, the dressing! These candied walnuts!" The woman tries to smile politely but she just can't.

Onstage, Reagan Arthur is giving a speech about the company's progress. The year-end, the highlights, this quarter and that quarter. She knows it all already. They've listed the speech on the program as being right before her award, and she periodically looks down, wondering if the order has changed. The order has not changed.

Two seats over, Bill has his chin in his hands, looking at Reagan like he's falling in love. She almost feels badly for him . . . almost. Bill was the person who'd been rumored to win. He'd had a vague smugness about him in the weeks leading up to the announcement. It floated around him like a cheap cologne.

Now she is waiting to be called, for Reagan to just finish his speech, to just say it already. . . . *Say it.* Silvia is still talking. Silvia is enjoying the wine.

She looks around for the cocktail waitress but it's hard to tell them apart. They all wear the same tuxedo and white gloves. The women have their hair pulled back. The men have slicked everything down. She's about to raise her hand when one of the waiters strides over, filling her wineglass.

It happens so fast it confuses her. She feels something flutter over her knee and she thinks for a second that she dropped her napkin. It's only then that she notices it on the floor. Sitting beside her right heel is a small white envelope. She turns to the waiter, but he is already gone.

She kneels, opens it. There are two lines of handwritten block type.

GREYHOUND STATION
HOLLYWOOD BOULEVARD

She immediately knows what it is. She has a sudden surge of nervousness, her throat dry. She closes her eyes to let it pass, her fingers going to the pendant necklace, to the small medallion she wears. She is still under the table, still holding the envelope, when Reagan calls her name.

CHAPTER EIGHT

IT'S NEARLY SIX thirty when you get to the station. Your hands are shaky. It's seventy degrees and you have the chills. You spent the night in someone's back shed, but you couldn't sleep.

As you walk around the Greyhound building you study everyone's face. You watch the woman sitting in the corner, a rolled-up sleeping bag beside her. You glance at the middle-aged man outside, two bags stacked on his suitcase, making sure there's nothing familiar in his features.

It doesn't take long for the cashier to notice you. The pacing, the quiet circling of the lobby chairs. He calls out from behind a clear bulletproof wall. "Should be out there in ten minutes. Space three." He points to the door.

He thinks you're anxious for the bus. You don't know what you're anxious for. Everything. The buses the night before were already full, but you were able to get a ticket for this one. Seven A.M. San Francisco. It seems far enough away to start again, big enough to lose yourself in. It feels like a chance . . . at what, you're not sure.

When you step out into the morning air, the lot is empty except for a few cars. Two buses sit in spaces five and twelve. Their windows are dark. Across the street, a club is just closing. A man is pulling a metal grate over the front entrance, slipping the lock in, latching it shut.

You try to focus on the vending machine, on the twenty breakfast options you have in front of you. Cheetos, Flamin' Hot Cheetos, pretzels and peanuts and Snickers bars . . . You punch the code for Cheetos. The spiral turns, pushing them out, and they fall to greet you.

You sit against the station wall, popping the bag and eating them one by one. You close your eyes and try to hold the memory again, the tiny snippets of the coffin, your hands, the church. As you walk forward you see the podium. An angel on the altar holds a trumpet. You remember the incense and that bright floral smell, how that one bouquet sitting beside the podium changed the air.

You remember, you remember.

Everything else exists in a hazy place, like you are looking through a camera that's out of focus. You can't quite make out the clock on the church's back wall. You don't know what you were wearing, what year it was or where it happened. You focus on the book that was in front of you, trying to remember the exact page number. You can't remember the passage. You can't even see the words on the page; instead the memory cuts out, your hand still on that ribbon marking your place. Still, you keep your eyes closed. You wait for it to return. With your head down, your shoulders against the station wall, the sound is background at first. It's somewhere beyond you.

You open your eyes.

You scan the empty lot. One side of it is all grass, some of it three feet high in places. A few tangled trees have sprouted in the abandoned plot next door. You watch the shadow behind them.

Then you hear the sound again: the quiet crunching of a person moving through dry brush. It takes a moment for you to process what you are seeing. The figure pushes forward and emerges from the lot. The woman is clad in a long-sleeve shirt and black running pants, her chestnut hair pulled back in a ponytail. She looks old enough to be someone's mother, the type of woman you'd see at a Little League game or in a supermarket line. As she starts toward the front of the building, you notice the gun at her hip.

You stand. She gives you a quick once-over as she doubles her pace. You turn away, starting into a run. You cross the street and go down an empty alley. She is right behind you. You scan the backs of buildings, looking for an entrance into the gated parking structures. They're all locked.

You go another block, but the woman keeps pace. When you look back, the woman is pumping her arms, her run effortless. She's too fast. You try to get a sense of her height, her size, wondering if you have any chance against her. You are only about five three. The woman is taller but she is slight, her limbs long and lanky.

On instinct you run in an arc, cutting down another alley and over Hollywood Boulevard. The traffic is sparse and you feel alone, exposed, the streets too empty to hide. A convertible sees you crossing and slows. It takes only a moment for the car to speed up again, racing past without much notice.

You keep going, turning toward the freeway. You can hear the sounds of cars somewhere above. For a moment there's nothing except that static hum, and it's easy to believe you've outrun her. But when you glance over your shoulder the woman is there, right at the last corner. She hasn't slowed at all. You try to keep your breath even, drawing long sips of air, but her presence unhinges you. It'll only take her a few minutes to close the gap between you.

You're all guts and instinct, muscle and blood and bone. You pull the pack to your front, unzipping it as best as you can. The knife is right on top. As soon as you have it you drop the pack, feeling the weight of it go. Everything you own. The cash. The supplies. The notebook. You try not to think about it, try only to feel how much lighter you are without it.

You pick up speed. As you reach the freeway underpass

you turn, moving down an abandoned street that parallels the road above. She's disappeared from view. There are bushes to your left and buildings to your right—another parking garage, three stories tall. You sprint along the backs of the buildings, hiding behind a Dumpster.

She is coming. You listen to her shoes hitting the pavement, the sound moving closer. You flip open the knife and clasp the base of it. *Three,* you think, trying to stop the trembling in your hands. *Two* . . . There's an unevenness to her steps as she takes the corner, and you hear her hesitation. She's realized you're hiding. She's registered something's wrong.

One.

You step forward. You keep the knife down. You level your right shoulder into her stomach, keeping your feet out to absorb the impact. When you collide everything in your body hurts. Her legs give out. She stumbles away, falling to the ground, her hand on her stomach. All her breath has left her body and she opens her mouth, wheezing, trying to get air.

Your first instinct is to go to her, but then she reaches for the gun, aiming it at your heart. Before she can fire you are upon her. Both hands come together in an X motion, over her outstretched arm. The force of it breaks her grip. Your left hand grabs the barrel and twists, freeing the weapon. You throw the gun as far as you can, sending it skidding across the pavement.

It stops your breath, how easy it was to disarm her. You

try to ignore the throbbing in your head, your shoulder, your side. Kneeling down beside her, you're so close you can see the mascara on her eyelashes. She is in her mid forties but her skin is pulled taut. She has plump, overdone lips.

One hand immediately goes to her neck. She pinches a medallion between her fingers, the metal glinting in the bright morning light. There's a man's silhouette on one side, an antlered deer on the other. She turns it back and forth.

You bring the knife up, letting it hover over her throat. You're not going to kill her, you know you won't. You can't. She stares back at you, her chest heaving as she struggles for air, and you try your best to pretend.

"Who are you?" you ask. "Why were you chasing me?"

The woman coughs. She still holds the medallion, turning it between her fingers. When she parts her lips, her voice is a sad, slow whisper. "I'm sorry. . . ." she murmurs.

"Sorry?" you repeat.

She closes her eyes, takes another breath, and before you can process it she smiles. Her palm comes up, hitting the base of your nose. The pain is so intense your eyes squeeze shut. There's only the throbbing in your head. She grabs the knife from your hand, your grip loose, your whole body weak. You can barely fight her as she rolls away. She sits up, adjusting herself so she has a better view of your throat.

She grabs your head with the one hand, watching you as she holds you there, the smile still curled on her lips. Then she raises the knife. The pain in your head is white-hot, your back scraped and bleeding on the pavement, and you know this is it.

You close your eyes, waiting for her to strike. You hear a whizzing sound, then the quick intake of breath. Something hits her in the side. A wound opens up, no bigger than a quarter. The bullet has buried itself just below her left breast. She lowers herself onto the ground, her body twisting and tense, her hand pressed against her ribs.

You stand and turn, looking for the person who shot her. You are alone in the alley. The buildings reveal nothing, the windows closed and dark, the roofs empty. It takes you a moment to notice the parking structure two doors away. A figure stands on the second level, beside one of the concrete pillars. It's the man from the day before, wearing a similar white shirt and black pants. You blink, stunned, as he watches you from above.

Then he lowers his gun. He stares at you for a moment, and if it's an acknowledgment, you're not sure of what. His face is expressionless. His hand wanders to his back, tucking the gun into his belt.

He climbs into the silver car behind him, slamming the door shut. You can hear the screeches and squeals of the tires as he takes each turn, winding down the parking structure, disappearing out an unseen exit.

CHAPTER NINE

THE FIRST KNOCK fills the tiny gas station bathroom. There's a pause, then more knocking, this time louder. You're wedged in the corner beside the sink, dried blood splatter on the side of your shirt. You have to get up, you know you have to, but the person on the other side of the door could be anyone—the man from before, the police. You only got five blocks before taking cover here.

Finally you hear a young girl's voice—small, unassuming. "Is anyone in there?" You stand, rinsing your hands beneath the cold water, dabbing your face with paper towels. When you meet your eyes in the mirror you look half dead, the overhead lamp creating strange shadows on your face.

You shake your hands dry. You keep your head down as you push out past the girl, no older than thirteen. Two hours have passed since the shooting, maybe more. In the morning heat you are all thoughts, wondering how long the man was standing there before he took that shot. Who are you to him? Why did he protect you? Why did he follow you, watching from above?

The world goes by outside you: the gas station attendant helping a customer with their credit card, a thirtysomething guy in a car, a store sign flipping to OPEN. Turning over your shoulder, the line of cars is endless, but there are no cabs, no buses, no easy way out. You scan the storefronts and office lobbies, the outdoor café tables and the windows above. It's been hours now, but you still think you see the man everywhere—in the passing faces of strangers, in the parked car across the street.

You're doubling your pace, your head down, when you recognize the intersection from before. It's hard to resist. The backpack can't be more than three blocks away, and without it you have nothing. No clothes, no water, no food. Hundreds of dollars are waiting for you there, the pack nearly visible from where you stand, the branches of the bush broken under its weight.

Cars pass. You check behind you, in front of you, beside you, making sure there's nothing you've missed. Then you start toward it, not stopping until it's slung over your shoulder.

One block gone, then another. No one is following you. Only a bus passes, tourists peering down at you from the top deck. Still, something's off. You can sense it. No police, no sirens, no sign of the man. You take a left on the corner, starting into a run, scanning the tops of the buildings, the parking structure where he stood.

When it comes into view there are no ambulances. The alley isn't sectioned off with police tape. Nearly two hours have passed and her body is gone. A truck drives up the freeway ramp, accelerates, and joins the traffic above.

As you near the long stretch of road you keep looking behind you, but no one's there. When you get to the alley there's no blood. You circle the pavement, going to the spot where you threw the gun, but it's gone. The stretch of open dirt below the freeway is scattered with broken bottles. You look for a trail, some indent or mark where the gun could have skidded across, but there's nothing. Leaning closer, you see faint lines in the dirt, like it's been raked even.

Beside the Dumpster, right where the woman was shot, the pavement is almost dry. Caught near the curb is a thin pink puddle, the stain so faint you can barely see it at first. In those two hours you were gone someone collected the body, cleaned the scene, and left. They even washed away her blood.

Staring at the parking garage above, you can almost see the silver car there. You picture the way the man stood just behind the shadows, under the awning, where he wasn't as easy to see. The shot was quiet. If you had been in a passing car you might not have noticed it at all.

You spin back toward the pavement, wanting some ac-knowledgment that it was real. Your nose is still throbbing. Your body is sore where it collided with her. You pinch your shirt between your fingers, studying the brown specks against the white fabric, the spray on your right side, exactly below where she was hit.

It was real, you think. *It happened.*

But when you turn around, the alley is quiet. Not a single car is in the parking garage. There is only that shallow wash of blood and the rush of the freeway above.

CHAPTER TEN

THE FOREST IS *quiet. The boy walks in front of you, his bent knife blade parting the vines. You stare at the tattoo covering his shoulder blades, the skull that stares back with its hollow, cavernous eyes. On either side of it are wings. The feathers are so perfectly rendered they look real. You keep focused on that, watching the muscles move beneath his skin, trying to quiet your breaths.*

The sweat catches in your hair. It drips in thin streams along the sides of your face. You grab vines as you move through, stepping over rocks and fallen tree limbs. The branch in your hand is heavy, five inches thick, the top of it sharpened to a point.

Somewhere to the right of you, a twig breaks. The boy turns and you watch his profile—the ridge of his nose, his thick black lashes and the black hair that falls over his eyes. He's seen something, but before you can turn he is yelling.

"Move! Go!"

You don't see what's coming, but you hear the rush of leaves parting, tree branches breaking, the breath of some living thing moving through the woods. The boy bolts out in front of you but thick mud sucks at the bottom of your broken boots, pulling you down. The beast is coming toward you, faster through the trees, and you are locked there, unable to move. As it approaches, you try to free your legs one last time. Vines snake around them, twisting, tightening around your ankles. You turn and see a glimpse of some massive animal, its fur dark and matted, a bleeding wound in its neck. The boy disappears beyond the trees. You are running, trying to move faster, when the thing reaches you, its jaws clamping down on the back of your neck.

———

12:22 A.M. You haven't gotten more than an hour of sleep and your heart is still drumming from the dream. You check the locks on the motel-room door. You check the windows, making sure they're still closed, the latches turned shut. You're on the fifth floor but it doesn't make you feel any better. You only notice the fire escape, the landing ten feet under you, the roof that could be reached with a ladder.

The dream felt so real. You can still hear the cracking of branches as the animal came at you. It was massive, its agile body darting through the woods. What was it? Where were you? And who was the boy with the tattoo? Even as you try to conjure him, his image is already fading, slipping back into the unknown with everything else.

You pull the notebook from your pack and copy down the

details—the skull tattoo, a scar that ran along the bottom of his back, just above his belt. His knife blade was bent. You write down anything you can remember about the forest. The air was heavy, the trees lush and tropical, as if it was another world away. It seems impossible, and yet as you write down the final detail—*an animal attacked me*—your hand finds your scar, running down the length of it.

When you're done you set the notebook next to the rest of your things. You lean back against the bed but your body hurts. Your arm bleeds, the scab pulling against the skin, catching on the rough, pilled blanket. The muscles on your shoulder and side are tender to the touch. At some point you scraped the knuckles on your left hand. They burn when you make a fist.

You spot the receipt with Ben's number, tucked inside the notebook's front. You think of his hand on your wrist, how his face changed when he saw the gash, wincing as if his arm had been cut. How earnest he had seemed writing that number on the receipt, pressing it to your palm, telling you to call if you needed anything. You're not sure if you want to see him, or if you just want someone here, if it's the loneliness that's wearing on you. You pick up the phone, dialing before there's time for more questions.

———

When Ben walks into the diner he smiles—this easy, everyday smile—and it makes you think of that word *carefree*, and what it really means. You are trying so hard to be normal. You've ordered a milk shake. Sitting in the booth, smiling back at him, you can feel the muscles in your face, how strange and stiff your skin is.

He chose the place—House of Pies—just a few blocks from the motel. It's mostly empty, but there's a guy in a sequined jacket and tie a few booths over. You've chosen the table in the back, against the wall, near an emergency exit. You feel better when you can see the entire room.

As Ben comes toward you his expression changes, his brows drawing together, his mouth set in a hard line. "Why are you wearing those glasses? What's with the hair?"

He slides into the booth and you can't help but be offended, your hands swiping at your bangs, adjusting the glasses so they sit straight on your nose. You've looked in the mirror so many times but now you feel like you missed something.

"I always wear these, just not the other day," you say.

Ben tilts his head, squints. "It doesn't have anything to do with that picture of you on the news?"

You watch him, waiting, realizing. He knows. Your eyes go to the door, out the front windows, scanning the street. You slide out of the booth, take two steps, but he reaches out for you, his hand resting on your arm. "I didn't tell anyone," he says. "I'm not stupid."

"If you know . . . why are you here?"

"Because you called me. It sounded like you needed help."

"I think I said 'Want to meet up?' What about that sounded like I needed help?"

Ben scans the empty booths beside you. You sit down, his hand still on your arm. He's lowered his voice and he's leaning in, his face right in front of yours. "So that's why you needed a ride? To rob that place?"

"I know how it looks," you say. "And I know how this probably sounds to you, but someone set me up. That person I called from your phone—they told me to meet them there. It was all . . . staged."

"Right . . . you were set up. . . . Okay . . ."

"Please . . . I don't need the judgment, Mr. I–Sell–Pot–in–Supermarket–Bathrooms. It's the truth. And now this man, some guy I've never seen before, is following me."

Ben glances behind him, out the restaurant's front windows. "He followed you here?"

"I'm not stupid," you repeat his words. "I lost him. I'm sure, otherwise I wouldn't have called you." You've been puzzling it out, and your best guess is that the man started following you after you went to the office, that he trailed you from downtown to Hollywood, where he saw you at the diner. After that, you're not sure. You thought you lost him at the record store, but what if he was there all along, following at a distance? Is that how he found you near the bus station?

Ben pulls the salt and pepper shakers from the side of the table, sliding them back and forth between his hands.

"Where are you staying now?"

"Some motel."

His nose is sunburned. A dusting of freckles covers his cheeks. In his hooded sweatshirt he looks younger than you, which makes his tense expression a bit funny, like a kid trying to play grown-up. "If you're not careful they're going to find you," he finally says.

"Who?" Just the word *they* makes you think of the woman with the gun, the man in the silver car.

"The police . . ."

"They haven't found me yet."

You glance around, making sure no one heard what he said, what you said. A pop song blasts from a speaker in the ceiling. You suddenly regret inviting him here, wishing you could have just fallen back to sleep in the motel room.

"I didn't do anything," you say.

"I didn't say you did . . . but why do I feel like you're not telling me the whole story? Is your name even Sunny?"

You pause before answering and it gives you away. He lets out this low, rattling breath, his forehead falling to his hands.

"I would tell you the truth if I knew what that was," you say. "But I don't."

"You don't know your name?"

"No. And I don't know the man who was following me, and I don't know why."

A man walks through the front door and you fall back against the seat, your hand jumping to the side of your face to hide your profile. He has thinning brown hair and a white button-down shirt. You watch the back of his head, waiting for him to turn, but when he does he has a beard and mustache. It isn't him.

"What's wrong?" Ben asks.

Your breaths are too short to reply. You don't realize your hands are shaking until Ben's staring at them, watching your fingers fold around one another, pressing down into the table to keep steady.

"This guy . . . you've never seen him before the other day?"

"That's what I'm trying to tell you—I don't know. I don't remember anything from before a few days ago." Ben knows there's more, you can tell from the way he grabs the shakers again, sliding them back and forth, back and forth. The waitress comes over and he shakes his head, telling her no, he won't get anything.

"So you're just going back to that motel?" he asks after a long pause. "You're just going to wait there until he finds you again? Or the police find you? What about your family? There must be someone looking for you."

You think again of the memory, the funeral, the few silhouettes in the front pews. Was that real? How can you be sure?

"I'm going to try to get to the truth. . . . I just haven't figured out how."

"What if this guy comes back?"

You shrug. You're not afraid of the man anymore, not really, but how can you say the truth out loud? That after setting you up, after following you, he saved your life. That a woman was trying to kill you, and for some reason he killed *her*. "Like I said . . . I haven't figured it all out yet. Or any of it, really."

You stand to go, dropping some cash on the table.

"Maybe you should stay with me," Ben says. "I'm supposed to be at my aunt's while my mom is getting better, but that fell through."

"What do you mean?" you ask.

"She caught me selling pot and . . . 'asked me to leave.'" He makes quote signs in the air when he says it. "Kicked me out Beverly Hills style. So I'm back at my house now, which is closer to school anyway. There's a bungalow in the back. No one will know you're there."

"I can't."

"It'll be safer than at some motel."

"Nowhere is safe."

"I said *safer*." As you walk he scans the room, the way you have been for the past few days. He glances over his shoulder at the back exit. You can see how it's changing him, how he already seems on edge. He's involved now.

"You don't want me there." But what you really mean is *You don't know you don't want me there*. There's too much you haven't said. It's not fair.

"It's just me anyway. My mom isn't coming back for another month at least."

"Where is she?"

His face changes, and you can see he doesn't want to answer, but you stay silent, waiting. "This treatment center just north of here."

Something in you recognizes it—the way he doesn't look at you when he speaks. His mom is sick, and you wonder if part of you has gone through the same thing. It feels too familiar . . . too real.

"It's just that . . . I'm in enough trouble," you say. "I can't be responsible for anyone else."

"I know."

But when you get into the parking lot he points to his Jeep. It's not a good idea, not even an okay idea, considering what happened this morning. But here Ben is, chewing his bottom lip in a nervous gesture, digging the toe of his Converse into the pavement, grinding down a few stray rocks. His face is becoming more familiar—you could probably picture it if you closed your eyes, you could probably hear his voice even if he weren't here.

You should go back to the motel, back to the impersonal room with the beige wallpaper and empty drawers. But when he shrugs and steps away, you follow. And for the first time all day, you don't look back.

CHAPTER ELEVEN

WHEN YOU STEP out of the shower the steam is so dense it clouds the air. The mirror is fogged up and you're relieved not to see your reflection. For once there is no scar, no tattoo on the inside of your wrist. You pull on the clean T-shirt and pajama pants Ben gave you, wearing your sports bra underneath so you don't feel as exposed. When you walk into the bungalow something is burning.

"I got hungry," Ben says. He moves around the narrow kitchen, flicking on a vent overhead. It sucks up the smoke coming off the frying pan. "Two grilled cheeses, well-done."

You get a second look at the pool house now that all the lights are on. It's just one room, the kitchen island jutting out, separating the couches from the stove and tiny fridge. The coffee table has been moved into the corner. The love-seat is folded open, the thin mattress covered with a few blankets. There's nothing on the walls—not a single framed photo, not a painting or poster. The furniture doesn't match.

"You don't use this place much?" you ask.

"Not really," Ben says. He pushes the sandwich down with the spatula, the smoke rising up around him. "When my grandma was alive she'd stay here when she visited. That's about it."

You go to the window, pulling the shades aside so you can see the main house again. The back wall is all glass. There's a single lamp on to the right, revealing a sleek modern kitchen, a few metal stools lined up in front of a counter. The upstairs windows reflect the stars. Beneath it, the pool is just a puddle on the brick patio, the lights out, the surface still. "So you've been living here alone?" you ask. "Where's your dad?"

Ben grabs two plates from an upper cabinet. He doesn't look at you, instead wiping the plates with a dish towel, working at them as if they aren't already clean. "He died a few years ago."

You want to ask why, what happened, but Ben's expression has changed to something you can't quite read. He sets the plates down and goes back to the stove. You think of the view from the altar, how there was only one bouquet, barely a dozen people there. You wonder who he was. The memory could be of your own father. It's strange to think this might be something you share.

"I'm sorry," you say. "I was just wondering."

"No, it's a normal question," he says. "It's just a sucky one. My mom's supposed to get home in the next month, but it's hard to know. So, yeah . . . just me for now. I turned eighteen this summer so it's not like they can do anything. No one can force me to stay with my aunt."

"I thought she kicked you out?"

Ben laughs. "You're a stickler for details, huh?"

He steps around you, reaching for a drawer, but the space is too narrow. For a moment his body is just inches from yours. His breath is on your skin.

When you finally look up at him he steps away. His cheeks are pink. He keeps pushing the sandwiches around with the spatula. You watch him, waiting for him to meet your eyes, but he doesn't.

"You could get in trouble for letting me stay here," you say.

He still doesn't look up. Instead he puts one of the sandwiches on the plate and nudges it toward you. "I could get in trouble for a lot of things."

"But serious trouble. Harboring-a-fugitive trouble," you say.

He grabs his plate and sits down on the edge of the sofa. He shrugs as he takes a bite of his sandwich. "There's no reason for you to be here, out of all places. There's no way for them to know we met, right?"

"I don't think so."

"Then we're fine. It's not like you're going to throw a party here, right?"

"No parties . . . yet." You laugh, taking a bite of the sandwich. It's the first thing you've eaten in days that didn't come from a plastic package or deli case.

"I'm not worried. You'll figure things out." He brushes the hair from his forehead. "Besides, it'll be cool to have someone here for a while."

He smiles, and you're suddenly aware of him beside you. His shoulder against yours. How the sleeve of his T-shirt brushes your arm. His pajama pants sit low on his hips, revealing a thin strip of his back.

"I bet it was the reward," he says, then takes another bite of the sandwich.

"What?"

"I bet that's why the guy was following you. The news I saw said there was a reward for information. He probably recognized you."

Your insides tighten. You're reminded of everything you haven't said. That's not why, and you know it, but he can't. "Maybe."

"Anyway, if they find you I'll pretend I didn't see the news. They can't prove that I did." When his eyes catch the light they're a paler gray, almost translucent. "So . . . *Sunny* . . ."

"Why are you saying it like that?"

"It's not exactly a real name. . . ."

Normally you'd be annoyed, but there's a playfulness in his tone. "Well, when I figure out my actual name, you'll be the first to know."

"It suits you, kind of. Your *sunny* disposition . . ." His smile takes over his whole face, and you can't help but smile a little, too.

You're going to respond, but then he reaches over and grabs your elbow the same way he did the first time you met. He lifts your arm up and studies the gash in the skin.

"It looks better," he says.

"Some guy I met at a supermarket told me it was serious."

"Nah. It looks okay. That guy sounds like an idiot." Ben's face is just a few inches from yours. "Hey, do you want to see something?"

"What?"

"Come with me. You're going to have some free time tomorrow."

He pushes out the door, waving his hand for you to follow. As you cut across the backyard you feel a little different, more at ease, and you realize that you aren't scanning the edges of the property or glancing over your shoulder. You're miles away from the freeway, from everything that happened this morning. The woman who tried to kill you is dead. You have to believe that no matter why the man followed you, he saved you. He could have killed you, but he didn't. You don't feel completely safe, nothing can make you feel safe after what you have seen, but Ben was right. It's safer here. *Safer* is the word.

"The key's right under this rock," Ben says, pointing to a stone beside the entryway. He takes his own keys from his pocket, opens the door, pushes into the back foyer. Dirty sneakers line the wall. There's a basketball, a jacket piled beside it, some books.

You're halfway down the hall and you can already feel how empty the house is. No music, no smells drifting in from the kitchen or comforting sounds of dishes clanking against the sink. It's silent, your footsteps floating up around you, a single light ahead revealing a bare dining table.

"I hate it up here," Ben says, and you wonder if he could see it on your face, if he knew you were thinking the same thing. He turns down the stairs and you follow. "I usually sleep on the couch downstairs. These were my dad's. . . ."

The basement walls are lined with arcade games. There's a row of ten or more pinball machines, a Pac-Man table, some sort of Skee-Ball game. Ben's clothes are piled on one end of a long L-shaped couch in the corner. On the other end is a blanket and pillow. He goes over, picking up empty Doritos bags, tucking a few prescription bottles into the drawers in the coffee table.

"He collected these?" You sit down at the Pac-Man table, taking a quarter from a paper roll on the top. You drop it in, maneuvering the joystick, but within seconds you lose your first life.

"There's this place in the valley that sells them," Ben says. "He used to take me there on my birthday to pick them out."

"How old were you?" you ask.

"I got the first one when I was twelve," Ben says. He watches you start the next game, how you can't help but get stuck in the corners, the joystick not moving as you want it to. He puts his hand over yours before the ghosts catch up, helping maneuver you away from them. You feel the heat of his palm.

"There," he says. "You're getting better." He lets go, his hand falling back to his side. Then he sits down across from you.

"You have the home advantage," you say.

"Prepare yourself." He laughs. "This is six years in the making."

He drops a few more quarters in. The electronic song starts. His eyes meet yours and he smiles that bright, all-consuming smile. "I'm glad you decided to stay."

The next game begins. The motel room feels far away.

"I know," you say. "Me too."

CHAPTER TWELVE

YOU SPENT ALL morning searching for information on Ben's computer. Nothing about a missing girl with a tattoo on her right wrist. Nothing about a woman shot by the 101 Freeway, no matter how many news sites you combed or search terms you used. There's no website for Garner Consulting. The news clips referred to them only as a tech company, with not a single name of someone who works there.

Now you walk out of the back bungalow, a towel in your hand, letting the sun warm your skin. The backyard is quiet except for the sound of the pool filter. You slip on the sunglasses Ben gave you and his baseball cap, red with worn, frayed edges. You're about to lie down when you notice a ripped purple hoodie on the patio, crumpled beside the last chair. There's an iPhone in one of the pockets. As you pick up the sweatshirt a wallet falls out. There are three credit cards, some gift cards, a

New York driver's license, and a Social Security card. You fan it open, counting the twenties in the main compartment—seven in all. You don't need the cash, but the cards are tempting. The girl looks enough like you, a teen with dark hair. You could use her ID and credit cards to book a plane ticket to another coast.

You're leaning over, about to tuck the wallet in your shorts, when you hear the creak of the gate. You slip the wallet back into the sweatshirt. Then you drop down on the chair and fold your legs to you, pretending to look out across the yard.

The girl walks over, her steps so sure and even you have to remind yourself that she doesn't belong here. Her thick black hair is shaved on one side, her bangs sweeping over her forehead, blending into the rest of her shoulder-length hair. You adjust the brim of your hat, feeling more protected behind the glasses.

"Is this yours?" You pick up the sweatshirt, holding it out to her. "What's it doing here?"

"I left it." She grabs it, tying it around her waist like it's not a big deal.

"You say that as if you live here. . . ."

"My grandma lives next door. She's friends with Liz? She goes up there to see her sometimes. She told us we could use the pool while I'm visiting."

Liz. Ben never said his mom's first name, but there are photos of her around the house. This morning you noticed a pile of mail stacked on one of the video games, bills and catalogs addressed to Elizabeth Paxton.

"I'm not usually one for sitting in a stranger's backyard," the girl says. "It's just . . . this heat is nasty."

"It's cool," you lie, trying to compose your face.

"Anywhooo . . ." the girl says. "Thanks for watching Rhonda."

"Who?"

"Rhonda." She holds up the purple sweatshirt.

"You named your sweatshirt?"

"I like to think of her as a life force. She was with me when I passed my DMV test, when I took my SATs, when I moved. First kiss, first boyfriend, first everything."

"Everything . . . ?" you ask, surprised at how quickly you match her tone.

The girl pulls down her sunglasses so you can just see her eyes. Then she smiles. "That's a pretty personal question for someone who doesn't even know my name."

"You don't know my name either."

The girl just smiles. "I wasn't wearing her, exactly. . . . But she was there. As a witness."

She uses her hands when she talks and her nails catch the light, the blue glitter polish sparkling. She doesn't sit, but you have the sense that she doesn't intend to leave, that she'll stand here talking to you until you tell her to go.

She plops down on the lounge chair beside you, her metallic pink bikini top reflecting the sun. Her jean shorts are ripped, showing the white cloth pockets underneath. She has a piercing in her cheek and a tattoo—a line of script down her right side: *If you expect nothing from anybody, you're never disappointed.*

"Your tattoo," you say, pointing to it. "Where's that from?"

"*The Bell Jar.* A book. When my parents found out about it they nearly shit their pants. They were all like, 'We can't believe you did this to your body. You're ruining yourself. It's so cynical, when did you become so cynical?'"

"It seems kind of cynical. But I like it."

The girl runs her finger along the letters, tracing a line beneath them. "That's the messed-up thing, though. I got this when I was thirteen. Three years ago. And when they said that, there was this part of me that thought: *Huh. Maybe I will hate it. Maybe I'll be one of those people who has this ugly greenish-black tattoo on their body and I'll spend years wishing I didn't have it. Maybe I'll have to get it removed.* But I still feel this way. I still think it's true. I almost wish I didn't."

"What about yours? What do those numbers mean?" She points to the inside of your wrist. It's a reflex, how quickly you cover it with your hand.

"It's stupid," you say, keeping it covered. She couldn't have gotten that good a look.

"Come on. I show you mine, you show me yours, right?" She flashes a smile. No teeth, just her lips twisting into a dimple.

"It's just something I got with a friend. The numbers are . . . his birthday," you say, wondering if it could be true. You think again of the dream, of the boy you followed through the forest.

"What are the letters? Initials?"

"Yeah, initials. We're not together anymore."

It's comforting, this story, how you loved someone enough to make it permanent. You almost want to believe it yourself.

She nods. "So you're with Liz's son now . . . Bud? Billy?"

"Ben."

"Right. My grandma had these fantasies that maybe we'd like each other, that maybe we could be friends while I was here. He's cute . . . a little mainstream for me. I go for more of the skinny jeans, tight T-shirt, is-he-gay-or-not-we-don't-know emo guys. I can't blame you, though."

You're conscious of the connection. This girl telling her grandmother telling Ben's mom. It's better if no one knows you're staying with him, that there's a toothbrush on the sink, some of his borrowed clothes crumpled on the bathroom floor. "We're not together. I just hang out here sometimes, but it's not a thing. It's just easier being here. I have to sort some things out at home."

"Gotcha. Yeah, sorting things out . . . I can relate."

"Yeah . . . shouldn't you be in school?"

"Shouldn't you?"

"I'm eighteen," you say. You can't be sure, but compared to her, it feels right.

"I'm taking a hiatus while I'm staying with Mims . . . my grandma."

"Where are you from?"

"Long Island. Have you ever been? It's a mall-based economy, if that explains anything."

It doesn't mean anything to you, but her expression changes when she says it. The girl looks down, picking at the frayed edge of her shorts.

"I haven't been."

"I'm just staying for a week, lying low, as they say. There was a 'scandal' at school. My mom's solution was to go online and immediately buy me a ticket to LA." She makes imaginary quote marks in the air when she says "scandal."

"A week with your grandmother . . . sounds kind of boring."

"Actually Mims is awesome. She does yoga every day and she's ripped. Seriously—her arms are more toned than mine. And it's just easier to be around her. I don't have to explain myself all the time."

The girl pulls her iPhone from her sweatshirt. She starts flicking through it, typing, then she turns the screen to you. "Wanna see something?"

You lean forward, watching as she plays a video. At first it just shows a kid in a supermarket aisle. The kid can't be more than three or four, and you can see her mother's legs in the background, facing away. It's silent. The girl wears a blue dress and she's dancing, though you're not sure to what. She shuffles her feet, throws a hand up in the air. Then an acoustic-guitar melody starts. It cuts to a woman who fits the description of Mims, caught in a moment by herself, doing a quick pivot across her floor. The video goes on like that for the length of the song, showing different people of different ages, dancing without knowing they're seen.

"Did you make that?" you ask.

"Yeah. I have a YouTube channel where I post them. It took me two years to get all those little moments together. I was constantly pulling out my phone, trying to record people. You'd be surprised how much it happens. That one on the subway—the guy with his headphones? That's my favorite."

"Mine too."

She tucks the phone back in her pocket, then studies her nails, picking off tiny flakes of polish. When she speaks again, her words are softer, slower. "The scandal was about the videos. My therapist would say I referred to it as a scandal to bait you because I want you to know what happened. I wanted you to ask. And maybe that's true."

"I'll ask. What happened? Was it that video?"

"No—another one. I'd show it to you, but my parents went through every phone and computer I've ever owned and made sure it was deleted. They hired one of those Geek Squad people. It's floating around the Internet somewhere still. They haven't fully wrapped their brains around the Internet, and what that means for my video."

"It was that bad?"

The girl pushes her sunglasses up over her forehead and leans in. "*I* didn't think it was bad. It started because of this photo that was going around school. I didn't know her, but this freshman girl texted a picture of her boobs to a guy she was hooking up with on the soccer team, and he forwarded it to his friends, etcetera. Two days later and everyone at school had seen it. And here's the thing . . . they hated *her*. Everyone was talking as if she was the bad guy, not him—and he was the one who sent it to everyone he knew. At a certain point I just got sick of it. So a few of my friends and I made this video—all boobs."

"All boobs? What does that even mean?" You can't help but laugh as you say it.

"Boob shot, after boob shot, after boob shot. Just boobs. I took video of my friends changing their shirts and bras, then I set it to music. Our faces aren't in it. The whole point was: What's the big deal? Why is everyone shaming this girl? She hadn't been to school for a week, and her friends said she wasn't eating and she couldn't stop crying. I was like: They're just boobs, people. WTF."

She talks with her hands, an animated cartoonish version of herself, and you wonder if she's someone you would've been friends with before this. Would you have liked her this much, would you have trusted her? Does it even matter?

"So it didn't go over well."

"No. Hence the trip to see Mims. I still think I'm right. . . . Anyway, what about you? What are you running from?"

Her wording catches you off guard, and even though you know it's just a turn of phrase, everything about it makes you uneasy. There's no reason the police would ever look for you here, but you can't help glancing at the back gates, making sure nothing seems off.

"Just craziness at home. My parents fight all the time. It's better to come here and get away."

"Yeah, it's kind of nice here. . . ." The girl stands and walks to the edge of the pool. It isn't as clear or clean as it could be, that's obvious, but she starts down the stairs, letting the water settle at her shins. She's about to go in farther when a voice calls out from the other side of the fence.

"Iz, come on," a woman says. "We have to meet them in a half hour. If we don't leave soon we'll get stuck on the 10."

"I better go," the girl says, splashing up the stairs. She leans over, gathering her things. "But I'll be around tomorrow . . . and the next day . . . and the day after that. No car."

"Me neither. So you're . . . Iz?"

"Izzy. Now you have to tell me yours."

"Everyone calls me Sunny."

"See you tomorrow, Little Miss Sunshine?"

You smile, and it feels so good it's surprising. As you lean back on the chair, the sun is comforting, and for the first time this morning, your shoulders relax. You know it'd be better if you didn't see her again. If you made up some excuse telling her why you won't be around tomorrow. It's more risk.

But as she starts toward the gate you say nothing, and that seems like answer enough. She holds the sweatshirt in her hand as she waves good-bye.

CHAPTER THIRTEEN

"COUSIN RITA." BEN throws the Jeep into park and turns the engine off. He hasn't stopped smiling the entire ride.

"Rita, really? How about Tess, or Zadie? Something cooler?" You pull the visor down, looking at your reflection in the tiny mirror. You've styled your bangs straight, so they sit right above your glasses, covering your brows.

"I think Rita's funny," he says.

"It's an old woman's name."

"That's why it's funny."

You look outside the passenger window. Kids stumble up the lawn, some with red Solo Cups, others pulling flasks from their back pockets. The driveway is strewn with crunched cans. Behind the metal gate, you can just see the top of the crowd, heads bobbing, the occasional hand thrown in the air.

"I shouldn't have talked to that girl today. . . ." you say, picking up your conversation from earlier. You run your finger under the leather wristband. Ben found it in a drawer and gave it to you, the strap now covering the tattoo.

"What were you supposed to do, ignore her? That would've been even weirder."

Ben grabs a few plastic boxes from the glove compartment and tucks them in his hoodie. "That news clip ran three days ago; if she hasn't seen it by now, she won't," he says. "I was the one who drove you there and even I had to play it back to be sure it was you. Worst thing that happens is someone tells my mom I had a girl over. She'll probably be relieved I'm not just sitting around playing Halo and eating Cheetos."

He steps out of the car, waving for you to follow. A girl and boy sit on the lawn, the beer sloshing over the side of her cup as they kiss. "So what's the story?" you say. "I'm your cousin?"

Ben laughs. "Yeah, sure. No one will ask, though. We'll be in and out in ten minutes."

You keep your head down as you leave the Jeep, your hand going up to block your face. The music is loud. The house spreads out on the side of a hill, the city below quiet and calm. Ben walks in front of you. He presses his hand into his jeans pocket, feeling for the tiny boxes you watched him assemble. He'd promised he was just dropping stuff off. In and out, just stopping by, he'd said.

He slaps hands with a boy in a Dodgers hat. You weave through the crowd, squeezing past girls with heavy eye makeup and stiff curls. "Rex, this is my cousin Rita!" Ben yells. A boy with bloodshot eyes smiles, nods at you. Ben pushes farther ahead, toward a set of sliding glass doors. Beyond them a few kids pass around a bong. Ben spins back, grabbing your hand.

"I'll be right back," he says. "Promise you won't get into too much trouble?"

"I'll try my best." You turn, taking in the packed yard. A boy has gone into the pool with all his clothes on. Now his sweatshirt balloons out around him, his jeans clinging to his scrawny legs.

As Ben disappears inside you cut across the patio, under strands of old Christmas lights, to a table covered with half-empty bottles. Two girls are there, squeezing limes into some pink concoction. You pour whiskey over ice, taking the first sip, enjoying how it warms your throat as it goes down. Ben was right. No one seems to notice you. The girls are talking about some friends they met up with in some park, how they go there to drink sometimes (no cops), and maybe they'll see a band tomorrow at the Palladium.

It's freeing, being lost among so many people. Some guys are playing beer pong beside the pool. Other kids are sprawled out on the grass, hair tangled and wet, their eyes half closed. You're wearing a baggy T-shirt, a hoodie, and shorts, and that's its own layer of invisibility. Not a single guy turns to look at you. No one studies your face. You sit down on the patio and take off your sneakers, letting your feet land in the cold, clear water.

You drain the drink. You watch the party unfold in front of you. The boy splashes over to a raft, resting his arms on it. Girls form a circle in the far corner of the lawn, dancing. You think: *This is what normal looks like.*

Your limbs warm, the pain in your side slips away. You don't know how much time has passed when Ben comes back. He looks into the cup. "Having fun?"

"I should've made one for you."

"Nah, I don't drink."

He's not smiling when he says it—the only reason you know he isn't kidding. "Why?"

"Because . . . I don't know. I just don't."

"So you don't drink or smoke. . . . Why are you selling pot, then?"

A strange smirk crosses his lips. He leans in, his voice lower than before. "Easy on the judgment, Miss I'm-Wanted-by-the-LAPD."

"Come on. . . . It's a fair question. . . ."

"I sell it to make money. Isn't that why most people do it?"

You take another sip of your drink, sucking down the watery mix. "You go to high school with these people?"

"They're private-school kids," he says. "I'm at Marshall High. I don't exist to them."

You don't know exactly where Marshall is, but it explains the drive to this house, how it took over half an hour, winding down through the narrow canyon roads, unable to see beyond the headlight glow. Now that you're out here you feel farther away from everything that's happened, from the worry that people might recognize you from the news. "Am I doing a good job at being 'normal'?" you ask.

Ben laughs. "Yeah, you fit right in. Do you feel normal?"

"More than I have all week."

"Usually I'll just stay out as late as I can after school," Ben says. "Kids go up to Griffith Park and hang out in the parking lot. Or I'll just drive around. But today was the first day that I actually wanted to come home. It was weird."

"Thanks . . . I guess?"

Ben laughs. "I meant weird, like . . . good weird."

While he was at school today you noticed the picture on the fireplace. His dad, his mom, and him, when he was around twelve or thirteen. They were at some formal event. Ben was dressed in a suit and tie. His mother was laughing, her eyes looking off to the side of the camera. They seemed happy, frozen in this perfect moment.

"When did it happen?" you ask. "Your dad, everything with your mom . . ."

"So many questions . . ."

"You don't have to answer."

"My dad died three years ago. He was ten years older than my mom and he just got sick. He had this cough, and he just kept ignoring it, he kept going to work. And then it got worse. Then he was in the hospital . . . and then he died."

"What was it?"

"Pneumonia. I was so mad because it was just stupid, you know? If he had just gone in sooner he probably wouldn't have died."

You think again of the funeral, of the church that existed in those few brief minutes. When were you there? Was it your own father? You want to mention it but it doesn't feel right—like you'd be comparing his life to some imagined life, something you're not even sure is real.

He looks out into the party, watching people push through the crowded yard, some holding their cups above their heads. "And my mom . . . I don't know when that happened. I know when my dad died she had to sort through all this stuff. There was a lot he hadn't told her about and I know she was stressed out. But then I realized she'd kind of lost it . . . she started hiding things from me. She was acting like a different person. She went in two months ago."

You move your hand toward his, slipping your fingers underneath his fingers just to see how it feels. His expression is more serious, and for a moment you feel tentative, nervous even. His face is just inches from yours.

Ben picks up your hand, squeezing it. He pulls it closer to him, treating it like some delicate thing, turning it over, pressing it between his palms. Then he looks out into the party, where a few more kids have jumped into the pool with their clothes on. One girl sits on the stairs in her jean shorts, her shirt and hair soaked, her mascara running onto her cheeks. "So that is the story," Ben says. He turns to you, leans in, smiles. "Any more questions? Can we just hang out now?"

"No more questions," you say.

"Good, then let's get out of here." He hops up, pulling you to stand. You slip your bare feet into your sneakers but Ben is already moving. You stumble behind him, trying to catch up.

"Where are we going?"

"Swimming."

He doesn't look back as he says it. You turn toward the pool, watching a boy struggle to get on a neon-pink raft. "Where? Your house?" you ask.

"Better," he says. "You'll see."

CHAPTER FOURTEEN

IT'S HARD TO see where the trail ends and the brush begins. You wind down the narrow path, your hands on Ben's back, your feet unsteady in the sand. Far below, the ocean is silver and shimmering, the moon casting light on the water.

"Just a little farther," Ben says. "It's right here."

The metal staircase cuts down the side of the rocky cliff face, dropping two stories to the thin stretch of sand below. You follow behind Ben, watching where he puts his feet. He avoids the rusted, broken holes in the metal, the spaces where the stairs have eroded. You grab onto the hand rail, holding tight, the other hand on the strap of your knapsack. In just a few minutes you're on the beach below.

It's a narrow strip of sand against a steep cliff, a few rocks rising up from the shallows. A hundred feet away an old sailboat is turned on its side. From where you stand you can see the coast to the south, speckled with light, a Ferris wheel turning in the distance.

"This is one of my favorite places. We used to come here when I was a kid." Ben turns to the water as he peels his shirt up and away, exposing his bare back. You drop the knapsack on the ground, pulling the thin blanket out and setting it on a nearby rock.

You take off the sweatshirt, leaving it there in the sand. Ben has already waded into the water, toward a small out-cropping of rocks. You roll the bottom of the shorts up, tie the T-shirt in a knot above your belly button, and follow, letting the cold water hit your ankles, your thighs, your waist.

You hold your breath, dipping below, swimming to where it's deeper. You're far enough out that you can't touch the bottom, but it's easy to move with the waves, and you wonder where and how you learned to swim. In just a few seconds you're a dozen feet from the rocks, their silhouettes cutting the surface of the water. The massive cliff face behind them is nearly thirty feet high.

The waves lap against the bottom of the cliff, where seaweed collects. It's strangely inviting, the way the rocks jut out, glistening and gold in the moonlight. Before you question it you swim over, hoisting yourself up, finding the handholds, climbing higher.

"What are you doing?" Ben calls from somewhere below.

You don't answer. The bottom of the cliff is dark and

slippery, the stone covered with algae. You dig your fingers into the grooves, the skin on your palms burning as you go another five feet, where the rock is dry and rough. It's so easy. Your body hugs the cliff. Soon you are twenty feet above the surface of the water, maybe more.

"Seriously, Sunny," he yells. "You're going to kill yourself. It's not deep enough to jump."

As he says it you reach a narrow ledge, no more than six inches wide. You press your body against the rock, turning around to face the ocean. The sky is right in front of you, spreading out against the horizon.

Ben says something else but you can't hear it. Your feet are already pushing off the rock. You can already feel the rush of the dive, how there is nothing below you, only air. Your arms fly out by your sides, your back arches. The water rushes to meet you. In that last second you straighten out, your feet kicking over your head.

When you cut through the surface you are so awake, so alive. Your eyes are closed and beneath the water, in that stillness, you have the sudden flash of a forest. A mossy ledge beside a waterfall. A figure passes behind it, just a silhouette. You breathe out, the bubbles rising up around you, and then the image is gone. You are there, alone, listening to your heartbeat.

There was no fear in it, no worry, only knowledge that you'd been there before. That place was familiar. It's coming back to you slowly, the memories returning little by little. How long until you remember it all? How long before you know who you are?

When you finally break the surface Ben is laughing.

"Holy shit," he says. "That was insane. How'd you do that?"

He laughs again, and you wipe the water from your eyes. You know you've done it before. When and where, you have no idea.

"I don't know. I just did," you say. The rush of it is still with you, your heart racing, your skin stinging where it hit the surface.

As you swim back toward the shore he follows, racing behind but unable to keep up. You hit the shallows and start up the beach. You stand in the sand, wringing the water from the edge of your shirt.

It takes a moment for you to notice Ben. He's frozen at the edge of the waves, watching you. "What are you looking at?" you tease.

He doesn't say anything. Instead he grabs the blanket from the rock. He drapes it over your shoulders, not letting go of the edges. "Just you."

"*Just* me?" you pretend to be offended.

"I mean, *you* . . ." He smiles. "Come on . . . it isn't exactly easy to tell a girl she's pretty, and cool, and . . . different."

"You haven't met a girl with no memory before?"

When he laughs his breath is warm on your cheek. "No." He says it softer, leaning in. His face is just a few inches from yours. "You're the first. . . ."

"No bank robbers in your past?" You whisper it, but before you can say anything else he moves closer and presses his lips against yours, letting one hand slip down to your ribs.

You let him kiss you, his lips on your lips, your cheeks, your chin. You bring your hands to the sides of his face as he pulls you to him. He presses his body to yours and you hold on to his back, feeling every muscle beneath the surface of the skin, rounding over his shoulders. He smiles as he kneels down, pulling you onto the sand with him.

"I'm glad you caught me selling pot in that supermarket." He laughs. His hand slides over your stomach, his finger circling your belly button.

"I'm glad I caught you selling pot in that supermarket."

"I'm glad you're glad you caught me—"

But before he can finish you shift on top of him, kissing him again, his words getting lost. Your hair drips onto his chest and you wipe the water away. He moves methodically, covering your skin with his lips, following a line from your collarbone to your chin. It feels so easy and good it's jarring when he stops. He pulls back. His fingers trace your scar.

"This is from before?"

"It was there when I woke up." You turn your head, covering the scar with your hand.

Slowly, gently, he pulls your fingers away. You close your eyes as he does it, not wanting to see his face. His breath gets closer, the warmth of it on your neck, and then his lips touch down. He kisses the length of it, not stopping until he's covered every inch.

"I hate this," he whispers. "You don't deserve any of it."

"You don't know that. I could've—"

"I do know."

He seems so sure you want to believe him. Maybe whoever you were before, whatever you did, maybe there was a reason for it. Maybe it can all be explained.

He falls back onto the blanket and you rest your head on his chest. You pull the blanket around you, nestling under his chin. "It'll come back," you say, not sure who you are reassuring. "My memory will come back."

"I know," Ben says. You lie there, the sand and sea salt in your hair, watching as he closes his eyes, as he gives in to sleep.

You want to follow but you can't. Ten minutes pass, then ten more, and you are too cold, too restless, thinking only of the notebook in your knapsack. You knew that you couldn't risk going back to the Greyhound stop, that they'd assume you'd try to leave again, looking for you at train stations and bus yards. If the woman was after you, there could be others. But who? How long before they find you?

You peel yourself away from Ben, careful not to wake him.

You grab a dry shirt and pants from the bag, changing out of your soaked clothes. You squeeze the water from the ends of your hair, tying it back, wiping the salt from your face. Then you pull out the notebook, flipping to the last page with writing.

- The man was wearing a white dress shirt and black pants
- He drove a silver Camry with no license plate
- He followed you twice: first at the diner in Hollywood and later near the bus station five blocks away from there
- He found you more than a day apart
- He shot and killed the woman who chased you
- He saved your life

As you read down the list you keep returning to two lines. *He followed you twice. He found you more than a day apart.* Twice the man knew where you were, appearing suddenly, as if out of nowhere. It's possible the first time was a coincidence, and that he tracked you from the first location to the second, but as you puzzle it over—all the hours that passed between the diner and the bus station, all the places you had been in between—it's that word, *track*, that stops you.

You grab the knapsack, handling it as if it's on fire. You empty the contents onto a patch of sand. Sorting through it, you separate the clothes, unfold the map again and squeeze it, trying to see if it's possible there's anything inside. You're all over everything, thumbs flipping through the bills, flicking open the knife blade, double-checking the canister of mace.

You're about to let it be when you notice the pack's lining. You cover every inch of it, pressing your fingers against the cloth walls. Finally, tucked behind the backpack's manufacturing tag, you find a thick metal square. With one slice of the knife it comes free, falling into your hand.

You can hear your pulse throbbing in your ears, your breaths so short they're painful. It's just smaller than a cell phone battery. You would've assumed it was a security device, something to prevent shoplifting.

You glance over at Ben, still sleeping on the sand, the blanket shielding him from the wind coming off the water. You can't put him in any more danger than he's already in. You won't. Instead you pile everything back into the bag and go, climbing the steep metal staircase, watching him as you start along the top of the cliff. When you get to the curb you pass his Jeep, instead winding down the narrow road that will spit you back onto the Pacific Coast Highway.

He knew where you were, you think. *He knows where you are.* You walk and walk. If he followed you before, he'll come back again, won't he? How long will it take to draw him out again? It's time you got some answers, from the only person who can give them. You'll have to set a trap. If the man followed you twice, he'll follow you again.

You keep moving in the dark, waiting for the road to split up ahead. Waiting to see if Ben's Jeep will speed past. You are still waiting when you hit the highway. You put up your thumb, and after a few minutes an older woman pulls over, offering to take you back down the coast.

CHAPTER FIFTEEN

THE MAN HAS been sitting outside of the youth shelter for nearly an hour. He has the air-conditioning on high but the car is still hot, the ice in his cup melted, the diet soda now watery. He looks down at the photo on the passenger seat. The kid can't be older than seventeen. The picture caught him in profile. His nose looks like it's been broken once or twice before. There's a tattoo peeking out of his collar, someone's name in tight script.

It's almost noon. He's sure he missed the kid going in. The only chance is getting him on the way out. It would be easier if he could just ask whoever's doing intake, slip some money to the person at the front desk. But there were specific directions. Park here, wait here, approach him after he walks this many blocks. The recruitment is getting more detailed as the months go on. Lately he can't blink without asking someone first.

He pops open the glove compartment. Beside the roll of cash is an open bag of Swedish Fish. Maureen would kill him if she knew. *Just one?* she'd say. *When have you ever had just one?* He pulls just one from the bag, folds the plastic a few times, as if that could seal it closed. Then he shoves the bag back in the glove compartment, hiding it behind the money. *There*, he thinks, shutting the glove compartment door. *I'll forget about them. I won't have any more.*

But as soon as he chews the gummy candy he wants another. He hasn't even swallowed it and he's reaching for the glove compartment again. The only thing that stops him is the phone, the stupid thing buzzing in the front pocket of his shirt.

It reads *Blocked*, like most of the calls do. He picks up anyway.

"Yup?"

"It's me. Quick question."

It's never a quick question with Ivan. He always needs to be calmed down, to be talked off some ledge. He's only been working for them for two weeks and the phone calls have been constant, these small requests for reassurance. "What? I'm doing something."

"The tracking device isn't moving anymore."

"Where is it?"

"Some park. It's been there for two days, hasn't moved even five feet."

"So . . . ?" He watches the front doors of the shelter. A short guy with a stained T-shirt comes out, a duffel slung over his shoulder. It isn't him.

"What do I do? I already gave them the second location."

"If you're worried about it, go check it out. In the meantime you should update them." Two other guys walk out, linger for a moment on the sidewalk, then turn right. The kid appears behind them. Shaved head. A sweatshirt balled up under his arm. He doesn't notice the car across the street.

"What does it mean? Do you think something happened?"

"It's been over a hundred degrees every day for the last week. She's in some park and she's not moving. What do you think that means?"

He doesn't wait for Ivan to respond. Instead he hangs up, tucking the disposable phone in his back pocket before he gets out of the car. He stays ten yards behind the kid, smiling because he knows it makes him look friendlier, more accessible. He wants to seem like someone you can trust.

Two more blocks before he'll approach him. He wipes the sweat from his forehead, turns the corner, away from the youth shelter. Just two more blocks.

CHAPTER SIXTEEN

HEADLIGHTS. THE SLOW grate of tires against gravel, then the engine cuts out, leaving the woods in silence. As the sun began to set you closed your eyes for just a few minutes, and now the woods are dark. There is a car in the parking lot. The door opens and shuts. A man types something into his phone as he starts on the trail twenty feet below.

The moon is full and bright, making it easier to see the bend in the trail where you buried the tracking device, just under a large square rock. You've been here for two days now, hiding in the brush and trees. You left Ben on the beach alone, and you know he's probably worried, wondering what happened to you, wondering where you are. But you can't think about that now. You needed to do this. If the tracking device isn't moving, you're not moving, and the man has finally come to find out why.

He is looking up, his chin turned in your direction. The faint blue glow of the phone's screen lights his face. You're perched high above, behind thick brush and shrubs, a few feet away from another narrow trail. You've hidden your knapsack in a ditch beside you, along with the empty water bottles and garbage from the past days, the wrappers from the sandwiches you bought in the park's planetarium dining hall. You riffle through the top of the bag, looking for the plastic ties and rope you found at an army-supply store. You feel your pocket to make sure the mace is still there. The knife is still at your belt.

He has his phone in his hand as he walks, occasionally looking down at the screen. You can see the glow from it, a halo of light winding up from below, moving toward you. You're just above, no more than twenty feet away from him.

He disappears, then reappears around the bend. He's moving toward the device when he pulls a second phone from his pants pocket. It's buzzing. He flips it open, answering it. "I'm here now," he says. "I'll call as soon as I have news."

You recognize his voice from somewhere, but you can't tell where. Was he in a dream? Did you know him from before? You watch him as he turns around, one hand balled in a fist. Whoever is on the other end of the line is saying something. The man's mouth keeps opening and closing to respond, a series of "buts" and "yes, buts" slipping out, and nothing more.

He hangs up, moving his finger over the phone, glancing

from the screen to the trail, then back again. He's within a few feet of the tracking device. He winces as he peers into the bushes, using the phone for light.

You step out of the brush, moving along the trail, winding down to where he is. His back is to you as he moves deeper into the bushes. He's thinner than you remember him, with skin so pale it seems ghostly in the moonlight. He's pulling some of the branches back, holding one arm up to protect his face, and he's so frantic you almost feel something for him. He seems like a different person from the one you saw in the parking garage.

His belt is empty now, no gun or holster at his hip, and as far as you can tell he's not carrying anything but the phone. You're only ten feet away now, so close you can hear his breaths, the vial of mace clutched in your fist, finger on the trigger. When he takes another step forward you spring toward him. As you approach you're suddenly aware of how small you are—he's a foot taller than you, and though he's thin he moves quickly, turning before you're even halfway there.

You shoot the mace, a thin stream of liquid hitting him in the nose and mouth. His face tenses, his back hunched, his hands covering his eyes. In the dim light you can see the sweat collecting on his forehead, moving in thin dribbles down his face.

When you're certain he can't see you, you move closer, pulling a plastic tie from your pocket. You get it around one of his wrists, shove his other hand into the tie and pull it tight, until his wrists are pressed together. He tries to run but he stumbles forward, his chin colliding with the dirt.

When he turns over his face is swollen and splotchy, the spray leaving a red stain on his skin. "I thought you were dead," he says, letting his head fall back against the rocky slope. "I should've known it was a trap. They warned me you were clever."

"I know you," you say, realizing in an instant why you recognized his voice. He was the person who answered the phone. He was the one who told you to go to the office building. "You set me up."

You unsheathe the knife, pressing it against the side of his throat. You want so badly to know—just to make him tell you something, anything, that is real. "Who are you?" you ask. "Why was the woman trying to kill me? Why did she come after me?"

It's only when the blade is against his neck that he tenses. Your fingers tighten around the end of the knife, and a familiar voice rises up inside you. *Don't. We're not murderers. We're not like them.*

The words are so present, so real that you turn your head, waiting to see the boy from the dream. It's as if he was standing behind you. It was his voice, you're certain of it, and you close your eyes, trying to conjure it again. A few moments and you know it's gone. *He's* gone.

The man looks up at you, barely able to open his eyes. "It was me. I never said it wasn't."

"Why, though? Why would you tell me to go there? What did the woman want from me?"

"I don't know." He wheezes the words, and it's only then that you realize your hand has shifted. Your wrist is now pressing on his windpipe. You release him, taking a few steps away.

When you turn back to him he seems frightened. His words pick up pace, each one streaming into the next. "These men paid me to set that office up, but they did it through people. There are probably four people between us. I don't even have their first names."

"You know your own name. Who are you?"

"Ivan. Ivan Petrovski."

"Explain," you say. "I'm listening."

"A month ago I was doing odd jobs for this guy. He was a friend of a client I'd helped buy a house—I'm a Realtor. He told me about another job his colleague was looking for someone to do. Fifteen thousand dollars for a month of work. And it involved putting a tracking device on someone. I'd report on where they were, and then I'd do some other work at the beginning and end."

"Some work at the beginning?" you ask. "So, making it look like I robbed that place? You *killed* someone."

"I don't know why they wanted the police after you; they

didn't tell me. They just told me to set it up and that as soon as you left the subway station I was supposed to keep a record of where you went. They've called twice so far asking for your location."

"Who's 'they'? Who are the people you've been talking to?"

"I have specific instructions from someone who gets instructions from someone else. I don't know, exactly. . . . I'm not sure who they are." He shifts in the dirt, trying to sit up.

"So you agreed to work for them, and you didn't ask any questions?"

The man shrugs, his expression uncertain. "I needed the money, and once I was in it, I couldn't find a way out. But I'm not a bad person. When I saw she was going to kill you I stopped her. I saved you."

"Who was she? Did I do something to her? Does she know me?"

"I don't know who she was; I'd never seen her before."

"If you don't know her, why did you shoot her? Why not me?"

The man squeezes his eyes shut. "I didn't plan on it; I didn't know that was going to happen. I'd given them the information about the bus station and then, I wasn't supposed to, but I followed you. I'd done everything they had asked for weeks straight and I was starting to feel . . . I just had this feeling something was going to happen, and I wanted to know what, what I was being paid to do. Then I realized she was going to kill you. And something in me . . . I don't know. You're just a kid. I have a daughter who's a little younger than you. I had the gun in the car. . . . I just did it."

"And what happens now? Are they after you?"

He keeps shaking his head and you notice for the first time the scar tissue covering one side of it, where his right ear should be. "I told them you killed her. I had to. . . ."

"Why? Why would you do that?" Your voice is uneven as you say it. All the uncertainty returns. If they wanted you dead before, what happens now? What will they do now that they think you killed one of their own?

He doesn't respond. It's hard to tell if he knows more than he's saying, but there's no reason to stand here, listening to him, trying to parcel out the truth. You kneel down, pulling a phone and the car keys from his pocket.

The phone is a cheap disposable thing, so flimsy it feels like you could break it in half. You go to the call history, pulling up the list of recent calls. Most of the list reads *Blocked*, but several down there is an actual number. You hit the button, sending the call through.

"What are you doing?" Ivan asks, studying you, his eyebrows drawn together in worry.

You turn away from him, bringing the phone closer to your ear. It rings twice.

"Esposito Real Estate," a man says.

It takes you a breath to respond. It's nearly nine o'clock at night, even later on the East Coast. Every normal office would be closed.

"I have Ivan," you say.

"Where are you?"

"Hang up the phone," Ivan yells behind you. You turn and he is trying to free his hands, his face frantic. "They know I'm here."

You look down at the screen, the numbers counting time. Without thinking, you hit the *End* button, letting the phone go dark.

"You shouldn't have called them," Ivan yells. He tries to stand, but he struggles on the uneven ground, his hands still tied behind his back. "Now they know you know. They'll come here—they're going to kill both of us." His gaze darts to the parking lot below.

"We have to leave. They'll be here soon." He starts up the trail in front of you. He tries to run but it's a struggle. His shoulders hunch forward and he keeps pulling his arms back, but his head is down and he stumbles.

You stand there, watching the park below. The woods are dark. It's barely noticeable at first, the lamplights lit on some of the narrow roads, the brush and trees rising up, blocking your view. But then you see the glow of the headlights. The black Mercedes reaches the parking lot below. It pulls in right beside Ivan's empty car.

"It's them," Ivan yells. "Leave both of the phones here. That one has GPS in it."

There's a steep path up the trail, to your right. You toss the phones in the bushes and run, knowing that if you can just get up that path you can cut back to the observatory. There are more cars there, more people.

You're nearly there when you notice Ivan, a crumpled silhouette near the cliff's edge. He's kneeling in the dirt. He twists, struggling against the restraints, trying to slip free. You're nearly past him, at the bottom of the path, when you stop. How can you leave him like this? If what he said is true, how can you go, knowing he'll be killed?

"Please," he says. "I don't have a chance." He is watching the car below. Two men have climbed out. They open the doors to Ivan's car, then the trunk, searching it.

You pull the knife from your belt and start toward him, cutting the plastic cord binding his wrists. He squeezes his hands closed, then opens them, trying to get the blood back into his fingers. When he looks at you his eyes are wet.

You both start into a run, taking off in different directions. The rocks are harder to climb in the dark. As you grab onto the slope in front of you, digging your toes into the dirt below, you see Ivan out of the corner of your eye. He runs down one of the side trails, away from the device, winding back to where it meets another road. He doesn't know this part of the park like you do. He hasn't been here before.

You want to call out to him and warn him, but he's already disappeared beyond the bend. He is already moving back toward the parking lot, toward one of the two men.

You climb faster, pushing up the steep slope. Your palms are cracked and bleeding, and you can only see the hand-holds above, the occasional foothold below. When you finally reach the top, the path empties out to another trail, this one snaking back toward the planetarium. It's only then that you look down.

Flashlights cut the dark, showing where each of the two men stand. One has already reached the device. The other waits in the parking lot. There is a loud, muffled yell. Then the flashlight falls. A figure runs beyond the trees. "I found him," he calls up to the other man. "He's here."

From where you're perched you can't see the other man's face. He wears a black baseball cap that shields his eyes. He kneels into the dirt, digging under the rock until he finds the metal tracking device.

He scans the cliff's edge, turning the device over in his hand.

CHAPTER SEVENTEEN

EVERYTHING IS IN shadow. The flashlight scans the ravine, searching for you. As it moves past you flatten against the tree trunk. The beam lingers on a patch of shrubs ten feet away. Then it disappears. You listen to his steps receding. When there is only silence you finally move.

The woods feel safe. Your body seems to know exactly how to negotiate the uneven ground, avoiding roots, ducking low branches. You take a steep hidden trail down the side of the cliff face, remaining in the brush near the edge of the parking lot. It's empty except for the two cars. The inside light in the Mercedes is on, the door open.

The man with the hat returns to the car, shaking his head. "She's gone. No trace of the keys. We'll have to come back for the car."

He climbs into the passenger seat. Ivan sits right behind

him, his chin is down, his shoulders hunched forward. He wipes the sweat from his forehead and you notice for the first time that they've tied his hands with rope.

The headlights flick on. The engine starts. The car pulls out and you realize everything that's going with them—any chance of knowing, any chance at the truth. You grab the keys in your pocket. You need to follow them. As soon as the Mercedes leaves the lot you run for it, not stopping until you're in the front seat of Ivan's car.

The interior smells of bleach. The glove compartment is open, its insides emptied out. There's nothing on the floor or passenger seat. It takes you a few seconds to figure out which key is for the ignition, but once you do your movements are automatic, your foot going to the brake, your hand shifting the car into drive. You don't turn the headlights on. Instead you roll forward, down the hill, barely using the gas.

You stay far behind, waiting until they're out of sight to make the right turn behind the Mercedes. The street is empty except for a few cars. You follow a pickup truck that is slowed in the right lane, moving when he moves, staying just a little behind.

The road goes on for a mile or two, and the Mercedes disappears for a few minutes. You keep a mental list of the places you pass—the Thai restaurant with the lotus on the sign, the gray-and-pink motel, the underpass and the two gas stations across from each other. You say the names of the cross streets out loud, repeating them as you drive under their signs, hoping to keep a mental record of where you're headed. *Western, Gower, Highland, La Brea.* It's not until the road crests that you see the black car again. It makes a left toward a low building with several barred windows.

Almost as soon as it takes the turn it pulls over on the right side of the road. You go to the next light, circling the block to approach the house from the other direction. Within a minute you have come up the street from the opposite corner, your lights still out, slowing to a stop when the car comes into view.

From where you're parked you can just see the Mercedes up ahead. The men don't notice you. They're too busy pulling Ivan from the backseat.

You cut through the neighbors' front yards as they disappear inside. Part of the house is covered with a tarp. You climb the chain-link fence, circling around to the cement backyard.

As you move along the back of the house, only one window is lit. It's so dirty you have to wipe away a patch of dust and grime just to see. Ivan is there with the two men. The house is mostly empty, the foyer filled with construction supplies—ladders and tarps bearing a logo for Parillo Construction. The dining room is outfitted with several tables. Papers cover every surface. Cardboard file boxes are stacked by the door. A map of Los Angeles is spread out on one wall, red pins dotted across it. Another wall is covered with a dozen photos. From your angle you can only see three or so—a falcon, a cobra, a shark. They're each labeled with cities—New York, Los Angeles, Miami. You try to get a better view but the only other window is on the second floor, too high to reach.

The man in the black hat leans on one of the tables, his eyes fixed on Ivan. "So I hear you've had an eventful few days."

Ivan picks at the rope around his wrists, his fingers worrying the cord. "I've told you everything I know about the murder. I saw the girl shoot her, then she ran off. I got rid of the body. That's it."

"What I can't figure out is why you were there when it happened," the man goes on. "It's just funny timing that you happened to be checking the tracking device when she was killed. Lucky for us, I guess."

Ivan just stands there, nodding, knowing it's not yet his turn to speak. His skin is already slick with sweat. There are wet circles under his arms. The man shoots a sideway glance at his friend, as if to gauge Ivan's reaction.

"And now this. You give us her location, you turn up there, then we get a call from the girl on your phone. What are we supposed to make of this? I mean, less than a month working for us and you're already fucking up."

"'Fucking up' is an understatement," the other man says.

There's a long pause. Finally Ivan speaks. "It wasn't my fault. She knew I would come, so she left the device there for a few days and waited for me. She wanted to know about the office building, and what happened there. She asked me about the woman who chased her. But I didn't tell her anything, I didn't. I swear." His voice is strained, his words rushed. As he looks back up at the men, a thin trickle of sweat cuts down the side of his face.

The man in the black baseball hat nods, listening. Then he steps forward. He leans down so his face is level with Ivan's. He's just six inches away, so close that it feels like a threat. "Tell us exactly what you told her. I want to know every word."

"I didn't tell her anything. . . ." Ivan scans the room as he says it, looking to the other men, his voice rising in panic. "She knew it all already—about the tracking device, about the setup. She knew it all."

"Did she know about the island?" he asks.

"What island?" Ivan says, confused.

The man asks so matter-of-factly you wonder if you heard it right. There's no way to know where the forest from the dreams was, but you think back to it. The lush, tropical trees. The vines and undergrowth. How the air was heavy and wet. Was it an island? How long were you there? Is the boy from the dream real? If he is, is he still there somewhere?

"One last chance. You don't have anything else to say about what happened to the client?" the man asks. "Nothing to confess? Some of our other clients are asking questions. We told them the girl did it, that it was all an unfortunate accident, one we hope to avoid in the future. But she's never killed before. They might not know that, but we do."

Standing crouched by the window, you try to make sense of it—how they tracked you only at specific times, how they wanted you dead. Who are their clients? Was the woman who chased you one of them? And what does he mean, you've never killed before? How do they know?

"I'm telling you the truth," Ivan pleads. "I swear I didn't tell her—"

The first blow comes from the other man. He was so silent you hardly noticed him, but he plows into Ivan, striking him in the side of his face, just below his eye. Ivan doubles over, his hands raised to cover his cheek, but the man moves in, hitting him again.

There's blood all over the man's fist. You wince as you look at Ivan, how small he seems on the floor, curling in on himself. The man kicks him in the ribs. Then he grabs the rope that binds Ivan's hands, pulling him to stand.

Ivan's nose is bleeding, his cheek swollen, a gash just below his right eye. The man with the hat moves in again, leaning down to speak. "Where did she go when she left the park? Is she still there?"

"She went south," Ivan says. The last time you saw him you were heading north, up the trail, there was no mistaking it. He is lying for you. He's trying to help you get away. "She was going toward Hollywood, I think, maybe back to the bus station. I don't know. She just dropped the phone and ran."

"We only have two locations for her—the station and park. Where was she the last few days? Tell us and we'll stop."

Your whole body is rigid, afraid of what Ivan will say. Was he checking the tracking device when you were at Ben's? You imagine Ben there, alone, when the car pulls up outside. You imagine him seeing the two men on his front porch. It was stupid to think that you could somehow protect him from them. You don't even know who they are.

You hold the keys tightly in your hand. You could get to the car in less than a minute. You could be at Ben's house in less than twenty. You could try to get there first.

But Ivan just repeats his story, his voice low and even. "I don't know. I didn't write down every location. I told you— I was nearby when I saw on the device that she was at the freeway, and I went to check on her. I saw her shoot the woman and I called it in and cleaned it up, like you told me to. Then she went to the park and she's been there since. The tracking device didn't move for days. That's the only reason I went there, I swear. I'm not helping her," he finishes.

The next few blows are louder. The man lets go of Ivan's hand and hits him several times, in quick succession. Ivan tries to protect his face, but already there is blood seeping through his fingers. It continues until the man in the black hat holds up a hand as if to say *enough*.

"I can't trust you," the man in the hat says. "And if I can't trust you, I can't use you."

The other man grabs Ivan's hands, dragging him to the front of the house. The man with the baseball hat follows behind. You press against the side of the building, lowering yourself down, out of sight.

Ivan had access to the tracking device the entire time. He must've known you were at Ben's. He had all the information—the motel you stayed at, the diner, the beach. He chose to protect you. And now what is going to happen to him?

You listen to the door open and close, to their steps as they circle the front of the house. They climb into the car. The engine starts. You don't know where they're taking him, but you can't let them hurt him—not after what he's done for you.

The car sets off. You count down from thirty, waiting to move until you know they've cleared the end of the street. Then you hop the fence, sprinting through the neighboring yards, not stopping until you're in Ivan's car. You pull out to follow the Mercedes. You pass the first corner, then the next, scanning the side streets for any sign of them. But there's only a lone taxicab and the neon signs of the passing strip malls.

They're already gone.

CHAPTER EIGHTEEN

YOU HIKE UP the trail, scanning the darkened slope for your pack. It was a risk to come back to the park, but without the knapsack you have nothing. You checked and double-checked your route, taking one of the upper paths, below the Hollywood sign, to make sure you weren't followed. You parked several blocks below the entrance. Now you snake down to the spot behind the bushes and dig the pack free. The mace is empty. The knife fell somewhere in the ravine as you ran away, but you can't find it in the dark.

You go back to the car and climb in, listening to the sound of your breaths. The clock reads 9:38 P.M. You pull the notebook from your back pocket and write:

- *The woman who tried to kill me was a client of some sort of organization*

- Ivan met these people through a man he was doing work for
- The men involved:
  - thin man with black baseball cap, stubble, 6'3"-6'5"
  - stocky man, shorter (5'9"?)
  - The house they used as a headquarters was off Hollywood Blvd
- Map and three photos on the wall: a falcon, a cobra, a shark (Code names? Related to my tattoo?)
- The men referenced an island

When you close your eyes you can't see the man in the black hat, can't make out his features. The other man is even hazier. Maybe he wore a blue shirt, maybe it was black. You left so fast you didn't get the exact street name. You didn't look at the house number and the Mercedes didn't have plates. But what they said . . . those words are still clear. *Did she know about the island?*

As you put the notebook away you notice a small square of paper in the center console, right under the emergency brake. You turn it over. It's a photo of Ivan and his daughter, no more than fourteen. They have the same blue eyes, the same square jaw and long, angular nose. Ivan's arm is around her shoulder. Smiling, he seems like a different person. Just looking at it your body is cold, and there's a tensing around your heart. Where did they take him? What is happening to him now?

You start the engine and drive, considering your next move. You'll need to dump the car somewhere, but then what? It's too risky to go back to the headquarters, even if you could find it in the dark. You don't know if it's safe to go to Ben's—the men seemed to have limited information on your whereabouts, and Ivan didn't tell them anything, but you're still not sure. You listen to the dull rush of air through the vents, thinking of Ivan's words. Why did they put a tracking device on you and then only ask for your location twice?

You drive for fifteen minutes. The traffic on Venice Boulevard drags on, cars inching forward, slowing up, then speeding down. Suddenly a flash of headlights blinds you in the rearview mirror. A black car is directly behind you. You turn. It follows. Again you turn and it follows.

You watch the odometer change, ticking out the miles. The car is still visible in your rearview mirror, even though you've switched lanes several times, even though you changed your route, trying to lose it. Has it been there since the park?

It's probably nothing, probably someone anxious to get home, but you need to be sure. Up ahead is a gas station with a few fast-food restaurants attached. You park at the edge of the lot and wait a minute before getting out of the car. You grab your pack and slip the photo into your pocket, heading inside.

The air stinks of fried chicken. A few people wait in line for fountain sodas. Others are huddled over their trays, wolfing down the last of french fries and onion rings. There are security cameras by the front entrance. You turn away from them, keeping your eyes down, heading toward the bathroom.

There are four stalls and you move past each one, pushing in the door, making sure no one's behind it. You turn the water on, letting it run until it's nice and cold. It feels good on your face, a stinging flush that wakes you. Staring in the mirror you start to feel normal again.

You push into the farthest stall, pulling your T-shirt off and turning it inside out so the logo is gone. You braid your hair to the side, making sure it covers your scar. The security camera has already seen you once. This time you'll walk out in the other direction, cutting through the side exit so there isn't a clear record of you leaving.

You're about to go when the bathroom door opens. Through the crack in the stall you see a man in a hat and sunglasses. He turns the lock behind him, trapping you inside. He's holding a gun.

You immediately bring your feet up, one on either side of the toilet lid, trying to stay hidden as best you can.

He pauses, looking down the row of stalls. He has a gray T-shirt on and it strikes you how ordinary it is, how normal. You still your breaths. You reach for the knife at your waist, forgetting it's gone.

He moves down the row slowly, methodically. His palm rests flat on the first door, then he pushes it open. He goes to the next and does the same. With only one more left you know he'll be here soon, in front of you.

There's no way out. No vent above, no way to slip under the stall without being seen. You keep one hand on the door, bracing yourself against it, waiting.

His steps are barely audible. You can see his boots—the polished black leather catching the light as he comes toward you. You take a breath, then another, preparing yourself to fight.

"Why's this locked? Who's in there?" a voice calls. Someone pounds on the door, the dead bolt rattling.

The man spins around, staring at the bathroom door to see if it will open. You can see the dead bolt turning, about to come free. The man lunges for the last stall. He is almost to you when the bathroom door springs open.

A man in a gray jumpsuit pushes in, an older woman behind him. "What the hell is going on in here?" he asks, looking at the man in the hat. Your pursuer's gun has disappeared behind his back.

It's your chance. You slide open the lock and push out of the stall. "He followed me in here," you say, pretending to wipe away tears. "He locked it and he wouldn't let me out."

You don't wait to hear the janitor's response. You don't even turn to look into the man's face.

You just run.

CHAPTER NINETEEN

AFTER TWENTY MINUTES, your arms pumping, heart steady in your chest, you finally slow to a walk. The man didn't follow you out of the restaurant. He probably got caught answering questions . . . maybe they even called the cops. You couldn't risk waiting there to see. You sprinted for as long as your legs would carry you, making sure you'd lost him.

You turn everything over in your mind. The man followed you, trailing you for miles, probably since the park. Who is he? How is he related to the men who questioned Ivan? You're certain it wasn't either of them. This man was broad-shouldered and athletic, taller than one and shorter than the other. You'd never seen the car before. It only had a slip of paper for the license plate, a shiny advertisement for Calabasas BMW.

Ivan said that they asked for your location twice. The first time was at the bus station, the second time the park. The man, like the woman, trailed you and tried to kill you. But why? What did they have in common? Who are you to them?

You're so deep in thought you almost miss it. You stand there under the awning marked LIQUOR STORE, staring straight into the glass case at a green bottle filled with dark liquid. It's the label that caught your eye. There's script, and above it an antlered deer with a cross in the center of its horns.

It's the same image that was on the woman's medallion.

You push open the door and head for the clerk, remembering at the last second to smile. He looks up and smiles back. He's in his late thirties, wearing thick black glasses and a vintage T-shirt. His laptop is open in front of him. He looks like he spends most of his time behind this counter.

"That bottle there," you say, gesturing to the one in the window, "what is it?"

"My sanity," he says with a grin.

You remember to laugh a second too late. "The Jägermeister," you clarify, reading the name. "Do you know anything about the label—what that symbol's for?"

"Finally," he says with a smile, "a real question."

He does a quick search and then turns the laptop toward you so you can read it yourself. You skim the passage. *Bottles feature a glowing Christian cross in the middle of a stag's horns.*

This imagery is in reference to the two patron saints of hunters, Saint Hubertus and Saint Eustace.

You look up and nod, but your whole body is shaking. You manage a short "thank you" as you head for the door. He's still smiling, still asking you if you want a bottle, offering a curious "customer discount." But your lungs are tight, your breaths so shallow they hurt.

You walk quickly, hoping the movement will steady you. It makes strange sense that they would want clues as to where you were and where you were going to be, but not access to the tracking device the entire time. It would make it more challenging to find you . . . to *hunt* you.

The man and the woman don't know you and they don't have a reason for wanting you dead. They are the hunters, you are the prey. You are a target in their elaborate game.

You sit down on the edge of the sidewalk, feeling your stomach twist and tense, running through everything that's happened since you woke up. How the men referred to their "clients." How the woman followed you beneath the freeway, waiting until you were alone in the alley to try to kill you.

Ivan had been telling the truth. He was part of it, but he never wanted you dead. He'd been keeping track of you for them. He'd used the robbery to keep you away from the police. He'd set up the interactions twice—first between you and the woman, then giving them your location in the park.

The man must've followed you from there. He is after you now. . . . He's still hunting you.

You pull the photo of Ivan from your back pocket, hoping he's alive, that it's possible they're keeping him somewhere.

A few minutes pass in silence. Finally you look up. Across the street, a police car sits in a parking lot with its lights off. The officer doesn't see you. As you start toward him, you brush the dirt from your knees and brush back your hair, knowing it's useless. You look how you feel—worn, beaten, half dead.

You keep your hand on the photo, running your finger over its glossy surface. When you're nearly at the edge of the parking lot the police officer looks up. He stares at you, squinting as if he's not quite sure what he sees. Then you wave your arm back and forth, signaling him. "Over here," you say, but your voice sounds so different now. Low and cracked. Barely a whisper.

"I need help. Please."

CHAPTER TWENTY

"IT WAS IN the afternoon," you say. "I don't know the exact time I woke up, but it was light out when I left the station."

"The report from the subway station put it at just before three P.M."

The detective has a gray beard and mustache. In his plain green shirt and gray pants he looks like he could be someone's grandfather. There's been no pounding on the table. He hasn't even raised his voice.

Instead he asks slow, specific questions. It's been like this for hours. He writes everything you say on a yellow legal pad. He keeps scribbling things down, flipping the page over, and scribbling more. There's a camera in the corner and you can feel that they're watching, that somewhere several officers are standing around, waiting to hear more from the girl from the office robbery downtown.

"We should have more answers after you're admitted to the hospital, but as I understand it—you haven't had any flashbacks? No memories that seem like they could be from the days before you woke up?"

"There are things . . . but I don't know what they are. I don't know if they mean anything."

"What kind of things?"

"There was this funeral. I had a flash of it. . . . It was only for a few seconds."

"Whose funeral?"

"I don't know, really. I was just walking past a coffin and it felt like someone I knew had died. That's all. It was barely anything."

The man nods. They took your knapsack when you came in and you still haven't gotten it back. You've mentally gone through the contents, hoping everything in it backs up your story, that everything, eventually, can be explained. You've told them about your memory loss, about Ivan and the way you were set up, the robbery he staged downtown, the woman he killed. The men, the house, that they took Ivan somewhere. Each time they asked why, what this was all about, you hesitated. You can feel the words on your lips . . . *I am being hunted* . . . but you can't bring yourself to say them. You don't want them to discount all you've said before. You need them to believe you, to listen.

"And the man, the one who said his name was Ivan? Have

you had any memories or flashbacks of him or the woman he killed?"

"No," you say. "None. Did you find anything about his car? Was it where I left it?"

"Yeah, an officer found it an hour ago. There wasn't anything inside."

"Can't you trace it?"

"The VIN number was filed off. It was completely clean—nothing on the inside doors, the engine, the steering column. We're thinking it was stolen a while ago. They're running tests on the trunk, but nothing yet."

He shuffles some papers, as if preparing to leave. You take a deep breath. You know that this is it, that you need to tell him now.

"There's something else." You clasp you hands together, squeezing the blood from your fingers. "The men who were at that house, the ones who took Ivan . . . he worked for them, and he was following the tracking device, but I think there's more to it. I think it was all part of a game."

"What do you mean, 'a game'?" The man stops writing, instead watching you intently.

"The woman who was shot . . . before she died, she tried to kill me. And I couldn't figure out why she would follow me. But then, after I left the park, another man came after me, one I'd never seen before. He also had a gun. He cornered me in a bathroom but I got away."

"And you think they were playing a game?" The man almost laughs as he says it.

"I know how it sounds," you say. "But it's the only thing that makes sense to me right now. Ivan didn't know what was really going on, and as soon as he started to figure it out, as soon as he tried to help me, they turned against him. I know that he set me up, but he's in just as much danger as I am. Wherever they took him, whatever he did—he needs help, too."

"We're going to try," the man says. "But explain this to me . . . why would these people go through all this trouble for a game?"

"It's not a game . . . it's a hunt. I think they're hunting me."

"They're hunting you? Now you've lost me."

"Please, just listen. . . ." You try to keep your voice even, but your throat is tight. You can't seem unsure. You can't seem desperate. "I think I'm a target. Like . . . prey. I think they dropped me in the middle of Los Angeles and that they set me up so I couldn't go to the police, not even after a woman came after me with a gun. I think Ivan tracked me and delivered my location to both hunters, first the woman, then the other hunter who came after me today. Ivan wasn't supposed to kill the woman; that wasn't part of the plan. It was when she tried to kill me that he understood what the game was about. He tried to stop it."

The detective is silent. You feel like all the air has left the room. He puts the pen back on the paper, scribbling a few lines you can't quite decipher.

You go on, explaining everything: the woman's medallion, the man who pursued you, the map and the symbols on the wall of the house. You mention the island, even if it's impossible to be certain what it means. The men referred to their clients, and now it makes sense, the service they provided. They allow people to buy entry into the ultimate high-stakes game.

The detective writes it down, sometimes interrupting with questions or to clarify a point. You lose track of time, but you keep going, not wanting to leave anything out. You finally pull the notepad from your back pocket, flipping through the pages to show him the details you've copied down. You know what it must sound like to someone on the outside. But it doesn't matter now. The truth is all you have left.

The detective is writing down a few last notes when a woman comes in. She sets two scraps of paper down on the other side of the desk, where you can't see them. She points to something she's written there, and then she's gone. She doesn't even look at you.

The detective—was his name Powers? Or Paulson?—studies it, turns it over. "Thank you for being so thorough. Anything else you want to include before we wrap up?"

The walls of the room are covered in some sort of

soundproof padding. You suddenly feel shut in, closed off. It felt good to say everything out loud, as if that confirmed it actually happened. And you've done your best to include everything—all of it—but now you're convinced you've missed something, that there's some specific thing on that piece of paper that you haven't shared and he is testing you.

"I think that's it."

He pockets one piece of paper and then pushes the other piece forward. *Ben,* it says. Then the number. It's the receipt from the first day you met.

"So who's Ben? You never mentioned him."

You try to fix your expression, try not to let your breath catch in your chest. "I didn't mention him . . . because I don't know him."

"You don't know this person? Then why do you have his number?"

It's possible they called him already. But you hedge your bets—it is not even six in the morning and you doubt he'd be awake, though it's not impossible. He could've thought it was you on the other line. He could've picked up just to see.

"He was just some guy I met at the supermarket. He tried to pick me up."

"Why did you keep his number?"

"I didn't realize I did. . . ."

You wait a breath, knowing that it's not the complete truth if it doesn't include Ben, but no one—not even the police—can know he's helped you. He has to remain separate from everything else. The night at the beach . . . the party . . . that kiss. You have to keep it all away from tonight, from Ivan and the men and this police station, this exhausted room with its cheery, flickering lighting.

"I hope that's the truth, because we're going to call it. . . ."

"I'm not lying."

When you meet his eyes you can tell you're losing him. His face reveals the hours you've been in this room, the story you told—the ludicrousness of what you claimed. You told him you were being hunted, like prey, by multiple people in the middle of a bustling city, sometimes in broad daylight. Can you blame him for questioning you? If someone told you this story, would you believe them?

But now you need him—to believe you, to protect you, to find Ivan—and he is glancing at the corner of the room, to where the camera is. Do they think you're lying? What was written on the woman's note?

"I know this sounds insane, and I feel insane," you say. "But I wouldn't have come here if I wasn't desperate. You took my fingerprints and I'll go to the hospital and I'll take whatever tests you want. You can question me again but I need you to help me. I don't know how I got into this but now I'm stuck. I can't get out."

The detective gathers the papers and turns, heading for the door. "I'll be back. Just wait here."

The door falls shut behind him and you are alone again. You tuck the notepad back into your pocket. You think of Ben, of the receipt, trying to estimate how long it'll be before you get to a phone to call him. He needs to tell them the same story you told them. He needs to explain the number away.

The security camera in the corner is still watching you, and as ten minutes pass, then ten more, you're concerned. It's the longest they've left you alone since you came in. You stand, pacing the length of the small room, wondering if it makes you look guilty. *She's restless,* they'll say. *She's nervous.*

You're asking people to believe you didn't do something you're on tape doing. You're asking them to believe that somewhere out there, a group of people are hunting humans for sport. You, possibly others. Then, besides that, you're only coming in now, after watching a woman die and being pursued by a man with a gun. You hear the detective's voice: *Why didn't you come to us sooner?*

Because you were scared. Because you were certain they'd arrest you, that now, days later, it's still impossible to know how guilty you are. Because you can't tell them anything about yourself—even your own name. You're trying to think of all the reasons, to understand it, when the door opens again. The detective comes in with a police officer. Her hair is pulled back in a low bun, her lips stained with a burgundy gloss.

She's holding something at her side just behind the detective, where you can't see. A wave of panic rises in your chest, and you wonder if there was anything else, if you've betrayed yourself in some other way. Are they arresting you?

She sets a cup down on the table and slides it over. It's tea. The tiny string hangs over the side of the paper rim, steam coming off the top. It's so innocuous you almost want to laugh. Then the detective hands you a map. "See if you can show us where the house is," he says, pointing to a green section of the map labeled *Griffith Park*. "Do you know which direction you went when you turned out of here?"

The pin on the woman's breast pocket reads ALVAREZ. She hands you a red pen. "We went right," you say, marking the paper. "And I followed them for a few miles. Eventually I was on Hollywood Boulevard." You trace down the road you think you exited out of, moving past the streets you know. Western, Gower, La Brea. You stop soon after. You went farther, but on the map all the side streets look the same. It's hard to tell where the turn was.

"You turned left off this road?"

The pen hovers over the paper, and you're not sure what this proves. Do they still think you're guilty? Do they think you're making this up?

"I don't know. It was dark and the cross streets were a blur. If I saw the turn I could tell you. It was after a gray-and-pink motel."

The detective and the officer look at each other, and it's a long while before the woman finally says anything. "You'd recognize it?"

"Definitely. You just have to take me there."

The detective nods, and it's all you need. The officer doesn't handcuff you. She doesn't say anything, just motions for the door.

CHAPTER TWENTY-ONE

"WHAT ABOUT THIS one?" the officer, Celia, asks. She can't be going more than ten miles an hour, the police car pulling around the block so slowly every neighbor seems to notice. A white-haired woman in a robe ducks inside, calling to someone behind the gated door.

"This isn't the street. . . ." You lean forward, your face just inches from the metal grate that separates you from the front seat. When she opened the back door you couldn't help but use it to measure how much they believed your story. *I trust you enough to follow this lead, but not enough to let you sit beside me.*

"But that restaurant I told you about—the one with the flower on the sign. That was just a little bit away," you add. "It has to be around here."

"It doesn't seem like it is."

The air-conditioning is blasting, but you still feel like your skin is on fire. "We're close—it can't be much longer."

She glances at you over her shoulder, and there's something kinder in her expression. "It's not that I don't believe you," she says. "If we don't have a crime scene we don't have much to go on. They didn't find anything at the park . . . not even the knife."

She points to some of the houses on the side of the road, another motel, a gated lot. She keeps pointing as if to say, *What about this? Does this look familiar? Do you remember this?*

The street was dark last night, your headlights off, and you were more concerned with remaining unseen. You only know what you know. But you're starting to feel like you have to turn up something, that there's no going back without some proof.

Her phone breaks the silence. She pulls over, answers. "Not yet," she says. "She thinks we're close."

Then there is a series of "yeses" and "nos." You strain to hear the voice on the other end of the line, but between the radio station and the traffic outside, it's hard to make out anything.

"I'll let you know," Celia says before hanging up. She tucks the phone in her breast pocket and pulls away from the curb. As she glances over her shoulder, merging into traffic, you look where she looks. Across two lanes of cars, you can just see a yellow house. It's set in from the corner.

"Wait," you say. "Take the next left. Try circling around."

She does, but she drives just as slowly as before. You circle back to the previous block. A low tree branch stretches over the road, a few leaves grazing the car's roof. You pass underneath it and suddenly things are familiar.

"This is it," you say. "It's up on the left."

"The one on the end?" Celia asks, her voice uncertain.

As you get closer, you see why. The tarp is still covering half the house, but beyond it the facade is burned black. There are two fire trucks at the curb. A few firemen move supplies from the garage to a pile outside. "That's the place."

She parks at the back of the house, where you have a clear view. The windows on the bottom floor are broken and black. The fire is out, but soot streaks the sides of the house, trailing up to the second floor. Through the doorway, you catch glimpses of the house's charred insides, the walls eaten away by flames. It's no coincidence. It couldn't have been random. They're covering their tracks.

Celia opens all the windows a crack. Then she turns off the engine. It's only when she gets out, clicking the locks shut, that you realize she's leaving you there. Your hand automatically goes to the door handle, as if trying it twice might open it.

Behind her, most of the firemen have gone back inside the house. One lingers by the truck, loading a tank into a compartment above. She approaches him and says something you can't hear. "Looks like a party," he says. "There's a bunch of broken bottles, some syringes. Probably just some junkies."

Celia disappears inside the house. When she returns, she's confused—it's all over her face. She turns back, looking around the back of the house, seeing what you saw. The place is exactly what you described to the detective. The house is the same color, the bars and roof the same. There's even the same broken patio furniture—two wooden chairs and a rotten table in a pile in the yard.

She comes back to the car, leaning down to look at you. She's about to say something when her cell phone rings. "We just got here," she answers. "It's the place she described. . . ."

You see now that she believes you, or at least knows *you* believe it. Why would you turn yourself in if you were lying? How could you describe it in detail if you weren't here?

She paces the concrete yard, occasionally glancing at the narrow path that leads to the front of the house. Then her expression shifts. There are a few more "yeses" and "rights" before she puts the phone back in her pocket.

She opens the car door. Her hand comes down on your wrist, pulling you to stand. She's squeezing your arm so hard it momentarily stuns you.

"What are you doing?" you manage. "What did they say?"

"They ran your fingerprints. There's a warrant for your arrest in San Francisco."

You feel like someone has rearranged your insides. You have to remind yourself that you weren't lying, that whatever she's talking about—you didn't know.

"Club Xenith? The arson you committed? How you bounced between juvenile halls? Any of this sounding familiar?"

"When? When was I in San Francisco?"

"Okay . . . spare me any more bullshit," she says. This time her voice is colder, foreign, and you can tell she's already back at the station, already thinking about bringing you in and telling everyone how stupid she was to believe you. She turns you around. When she reaches for the handcuffs at her waist you don't initially resist. She nearly has them on you when you pull away, slipping from her grasp.

She looks surprised. As you spin back, heading toward the neighbor's backyard, she grabs for her radio. You dig your toe into the chain-link fence, jumping it, and land hard on the other side. You expect her to come running after you, but when you turn back she's still by the car. She's still standing there, the radio to her lips, calling to someone on the other end.

CHAPTER TWENTY-TWO

WHEN THE POLICE come to Ben's door he's still asleep, the bell sounding somewhere above, like some strange, distant song. He twists on the couch, pulls the blanket to his neck. He keeps his eyes closed but then they knock several times, banging hard against the wood.

He's up. Wiping the crust from his eyes, his legs feeling unsteady as he fumbles in the dark basement. He trips over his shoes. As he goes to the stairs the knocking is louder, barreling toward him down the long hall. He knows something's wrong. He stands there in the foyer, his skin cold and clammy, wondering if it's too late to run.

He stares through the peephole. Two uniformed men stare back.

The cop has his badge out already. He holds it in front of the peephole, waiting. "LAPD," he says. They heard footsteps in the hall. The officers already know he's there.

Ben turns back into the house, making a list of where everything is—the pound he has in the coffee table in the basement, the plastic boxes and scale in his closet. When he opens the door he still pretends to be half asleep, even though his heart is wild in his chest, his hands shaky. He's in his boxers. He wipes his eyes again, wipes his nose. "Can I help you?"

It's about his mom. They know he's been selling pot. They caught him on camera with Sunny somewhere and now they're here, looking for her. He doesn't consider the other option. He won't consider that someone could be dead.

"Morning . . . Ben Paxton?"

"Yeah . . ."

"Are your parents home?"

"No, my mom's not here . . . why?"

"We were hoping to ask you some questions. Do you have a minute?"

"Sure, yeah."

The first cop is older, with black hair that's stiff with gel. He holds up a piece of paper. Ben takes it, turns it over, and studies the receipt before understanding what it is.

"Does that look familiar?"

"It's my phone number," Ben says. "I wrote it down for someone."

"Who?" The younger officer is heavier, balding at his temples. Ben doesn't know whether to lie about her or to tell the truth. Where did they find this? What do they know? If they had any reason to think she'd stayed here he'd already be in trouble. Wouldn't they be asking to come in?

"A girl I met at the supermarket."

The officer plucks the receipt out of Ben's hand, folds it, then puts it back in his pocket. "When did you meet her?"

"About a week ago. Why?"

"Did she call?" the older officer asks.

Do they know? Ben tries to figure out where Sunny called him from . . . the motel? Do they know she was there?

"No, she never called. Why, what happened?"

"We're investigating a case she's involved in." Ben waits, wants the younger officer to say more, but he doesn't. What case? Where is she? He wants to ask but he's afraid he'll give something away.

"Is she okay?" It's all he can manage. The officer pauses, like he's puzzling over the question, and Ben feels the need to say more, to explain. "When I met her she seemed kind of out of it. That's why I gave her my number."

"What do you mean, 'out of it'?"

"Just, I don't know. She had a cut on her arm." It sounds so stupid when he says it out loud. Why would he care about a stranger? He should stop talking; he shouldn't say anything else.

"If you hear from her, you'll let us know." It's part question, part statement.

"Sure, yeah. I will."

Ben's afraid they might ask something else, that maybe they'll want to come in, but those few simple answers seem to appease them. The older one turns to go first, the younger one following, and they whisper something to each other as they start down the front path. Ben watches them get into the car.

He closes the door, locks it. He keeps his face to the peephole, forehead resting against the wood. They're sitting in the car. It takes them a few minutes to start it, to pull away.

They don't know anything, Ben reminds himself. They were just checking in. *You're fine; it's fine.* But as he stares out at the empty street his breaths are still shallow. His hands feel numb. Then two questions consume him, one after the other:

Where is she? Where did she go?

CHAPTER TWENTY-THREE

WHEN BEN ANSWERS the door the Dodgers game is on in the background. He's in sweatpants and a T-shirt, his hair messy, as if he'd just rolled out of bed. Behind him, two boys are on the living room couch. They're scrawny, their chins covered with stubble. One has a backward hat on and acne on his cheeks. The other is rolling a joint. They barely look up.

Ben's eyes squeeze shut, as if you've just thrown water in his face. Before you can say anything he pulls you away from them, into the dining room, shutting the door behind him. You know it's better if they don't see you.

"Where were you? Do you know the cops are looking for you?"

"They've always been looking for me."

Ben shakes his head, points out the front window. "No,

they were *here*. This morning. They came here and wanted to know if you'd called me."

"Shit." You let out a deep breath, thinking of the receipt they found in the backpack. You wanted to warn Ben they might contact him, but after you ran from Officer Alvarez you were trapped on the hillside above Franklin, police cars trailing the street below. You hid behind someone's shed, waiting until the streets were clear to make your way back east. All you have now is the notepad, the folded picture of Ivan, and the T-shirt and shorts you've been wearing for days. "What did you say?"

"I said you never called me, which . . . was the right answer? What was I supposed to say?"

He goes to the front window, looking out on the street. You can't help but second-guess yourself now. You knew they would call him, but it's another thing for them to show up asking questions. You'd watched the street before you approached the house. Is it possible you missed a parked car with someone in it? Is there someone outside now, watching?

He glances over his shoulder, listening to his friends in the other room. "I'm sorry," you say. "I had nowhere else to go."

He looks down at your ripped shorts and sneakers, which are still filthy. Orange dust coats your skin and hair. "Where have you been? Where's your backpack?"

"It's gone."

Ben brushes his hair off his forehead and you can tell he's

thinking it through. He sucks in a breath before he speaks. "You left me alone on that beach. I woke up and I had no idea what happened to you, I had no idea where you went. Now you're back . . . because you need somewhere to crash? Is that it?"

"No, that's not it."

"That's what you just said. . . ."

You consider it. There's no more money, no more supplies—everything you had is gone. But you didn't have to come here. You walked an extra mile and a half, past a park and a schoolyard you could've hid in, kept going even when two police cars pulled onto the street in front of you.

"I came because I trust you," you say.

Ben rests his hand against the doorframe. He stares at the carpet for a few breaths and you wonder if there's something more you can say. You're not trying to convince him—it's the truth.

After a long silence he opens the door a crack, looking into the hall. Then he points to one of the chairs around the dining table. "Just give me a few minutes to get them out of here."

He disappears back into the living room. You sit and wait, listening to the television turn off, to the boys' quiet, confused questions. It's not until they're outside, the door shut behind them, that Ben waves you back in.

The living room is a mess. The coffee table is covered

in potato-chip crumbs and empty Doritos bags. There are a few Red Bull concoctions in glasses, the electric-yellow liquid mixing with half-melted ice cubes. A few plastic containers filled with pot.

You sit down on the couch, letting the cushions envelop you. Ben moves around you, picking up the empty cans on the floor. A minute passes, maybe two, before he says anything. "Come on, I know you probably don't want to talk about it, but you have to. You disappeared on me and the next thing I know the cops are at my door. What the hell? What am I supposed to think?"

You lean in, cradling your head in your hands, not sure if you can bring yourself to do it. If you tell him what happened—today, yesterday, the day before—it makes it more real.

"I went to the police . . . and they didn't believe me."

The words stop him. "Did you tell them about the man who followed you? And your memory?"

"Everything," you say. *Much more than I've told you.*

"Why didn't they believe you?"

Ben is standing there, waiting, wondering how they could possibly turn you away. His eyes are so kind, so willing to see the best in you, that you know you can't stay here another minute without telling him everything that happened. He deserves to know the danger, to weigh it as you have. You owe him that much.

You look down as you say it, telling him about the woman with the gun, how Ivan killed her beneath the freeway. About the tracking device and why you needed to leave him that night on the beach. About the house and the man who followed you from the park. You finish with the only conclusion you've come to, the way you've connected the dots. You're a pawn in some real-life game, a piece of prey, a target to be killed.

Ben just sits there, staring at a spot behind you, quietly processing everything. After a moment he gets up and starts pacing back and forth behind the couch. Finally he speaks. "So you told the police all of this, and what? They think you just made it up?"

"They still think I'm responsible for that robbery downtown. They don't believe me, because they don't trust me. And they don't trust me because apparently I have a record. Arson." You don't look at him as you say it. "I don't know all the details. I need your computer. . . ."

Ben nods, still looking numb. He seems to be glad to be doing something, anything, as he retrieves the laptop from downstairs. He hands it to you without a word. You sit down on the couch, flipping it open, glad to have something to look at other than his shocked, confused face.

You open up a search and type in *Club Xenith, San Francisco*. There are five links just on the first page.

Fire Was Arson, SFPD Says

Fire at Club Xenith Ruled Arson

Homeless Teens Might Be Responsible for SF Arson Case

You immediately go to the third link down, clicking through to an article on the fire. It mentions that it was set with alcohol. A group of teenagers who'd been living in Golden Gate Park are suspected, and a few have been arrested before for thefts around the Haight, though no names are mentioned.

You turn the screen to face Ben, waiting for him to read through it.

"They knew this," you say. "The people who are running this thing. They know I have a record, and that's why they set the fire at the house the way they did. They made it look like some party, knowing that if I went to the police they'd find my record. They'd just assume it was more of the same."

You keep staring at the last headline, *Homeless Teens Might Be Responsible for SF Arson Case*. You've been waiting to find out something, anything about yourself, but there's no relief in this.

"I'm nobody," you say. "No one is looking for me. There's no family waiting for me at home. Was that why they chose me? They thought they'd kill me, and no one would ever know or care?"

Ben doesn't respond. You can feel his eyes on you, but you can't look at him, not yet. Just saying it tightens your throat. As you stare at the table, the cans, the crumpled candy wrappers, the room is uncertain through a wash of sudden tears.

He takes a few steps toward you, sitting beside you on the

couch, lowering his head until he's in your view. "That's not true. I care."

He pulls you to him and it feels so good and easy, your arms wrapping around his shoulders, slinging your legs over his lap. You tilt your chin up toward him, your lips just inches apart. His eyes meet yours. It's the feeling of falling, the same weightlessness you knew when your feet left the cliff. Nothing you can do can stop it now. His hands are in your hair, slowly slipping down along your jaw.

Two breaths, then three. His grip tightens. You can feel his body tense, can hear his lungs beneath his ribs, the shortness as he takes in air. In an instant his mouth is right against yours. He kisses you hard, his tongue running along your bottom lip. Then he buries his face in your neck.

You lie back, stretching out along the length of the couch. He sets himself beside you, one arm resting beneath your head. Your shirt comes off with just a few tugs. Your sports bra peeled up and over. Your skin is exposed. Then you feel his hands on you. They slide up your stomach, lingering for a moment on your ribs.

Your lips find his. You pull away and he is watching you, letting his gaze drop to your collarbone, to your chest, to your stomach. His hair falls over his forehead, his cheeks are flushed. His mouth on yours, and everything is a reminder that you are here, with him. There's nowhere else for you to go.

CHAPTER TWENTY-FOUR

THE BOY IS there, lying beside you, his fingers against your chin. He brushes his thumb over your bottom lip, leaving it there. He studies your features, his brown eyes scanning back and forth, taking everything in.

Light streams down through the leaves. His upper lip dips in a deep V. He has two tiny beauty marks on his right cheekbone, just below his eye. His forehead is scraped and bruised, but somehow he still looks perfect.

He moves his thumb away, pressing his lips to yours. At first he kisses you gently, barely touching you as his fingers sweep over your cheekbone, your eyebrow, your hair. He shifts on top of you. His elbows rest on either side of your head and he kisses you again, harder this time, pushing you deeper into the leaves and moss. He is saying something you can't hear, his words muffled on your skin, lost in your tangled hair.

You move your hands over his bare back, feeling the muscles above his shoulder blades. You lift your head, stretching toward him, but everywhere you go his lips find you, touching down on your cheeks, your neck. "I won't let them hurt you," he whispers. "I can't lose you."

When you meet his gaze his eyes are wet. He pulls you up, into his lap, your legs wrapping around his waist. "I won't, I can't," he says.

It's hard to breathe, your mouth on his, your hands holding on to his shoulders, pulling yourself closer.

When your eyes tear up it's not because you're not safe with him and you never will be. It's not because you'll die beneath these trees. It's because you know now that it doesn't matter. He is here and he loves you, and because of that you are no longer afraid.

"He'll be here soon," you say. "You have to go, you have to—"

———

Someone grabs your shoulder, startling you. The room comes into focus around you. Sunlight floods in through the window as you take in the clutter on the coffee table from the night before.

"What's wrong?" Ben asks, leaning over the couch. "You were saying something in your sleep. You looked like you were crying. . . ."

You rub the tears from your eyes. "What time is it?"

"Almost noon." Ben squeezes onto the edge of the couch, resting his hand on yours.

"What was I saying?"

"I couldn't make it out. . . ."

You sit up, remembering that you're wearing Ben's T-shirt and pajama pants. You took a shower late last night, before you went to sleep, and your hair is still damp and tangled in places. "I'm fine; it was just a dream. Give me a minute?"

Ben kisses you on the forehead, then disappears downstairs. You go to the armchair in the corner, pulling the notepad from the back pocket of your shorts, a pen that fell on the floor. You fold down a blank page and write.

- The boy from the island was being hunted
- The hunter was a man

You think through the rest of the dream, trying to decipher the details of it, if there was anything identifying about the flowers or the trees, anything to help you know where or when it was. But nothing stands out. The boy was the most vivid thing there.

You flip back to the pages before, where you've written every detail of your encounter with the man with the gun. You've copied down the symbol from the liquor bottle. Saint Eustace, one of the patron saints of hunters. Ivan's photo is tucked beside it, now fogged with fingerprints. You stare at it, hoping he's still alive. When you set the trap you didn't know who he was or what he wanted. You didn't know what would happen next. You know he's in danger, you're certain he is, but how can you help him?

As you search back through the notes on the house, you think again of the room. The tarps, the ladders, the boxes with the logo on the side. The image is so vivid. You grab Ben's laptop where you left it last night and type in *Parillo Construction*, pulling up an address. It's less than a half hour away.

Downstairs, Ben is hovering over one of the pinball machines. He leans in, pressing the buttons on the sides.

"Have to keep my high score up; you're inching closer," he says.

"I only played a few times."

"I know . . . you're that good." He smiles, and you know he's trying to lighten the mood. You lean on the edge of the machine as the ball shoots up and around.

"I need to borrow your car."

"What? Where are you going?"

"I just realized that I didn't tell the police everything. There were these construction materials I saw at the house, and they had a logo on them. I can explain it all later."

"Okay," Ben says. His voice sounds breezy enough, but his hands drop to his sides.

"Don't worry, I'll be careful."

Ben just laughs as he goes to get his keys. He holds them in his hand, staring at them. You're waiting for him to pass them over when he finally speaks. "You really think I'm handing my car over to a known criminal?"

You can't help the smile that fights its way to the corner of your lips. For the first time, you feel less alone. "That's a really bad idea, Ben."

"Look, you're going to need someone there to call the police if someone comes after you again, or to—"

"The police don't care, Ben."

He closes his fingers around the key chain, hiding it. He just stands there, waiting for you to say something. You know it's a terrible idea. It's wrong to let him get any more involved than he already is.

"Fine," you say. "I'll ride shotgun."

CHAPTER TWENTY-FIVE

THE STREET IS a mix of run-down bungalows, strip malls, and empty lots. As you approach the address listed for Parillo Construction, you scan the sidewalk, looking for anything that seems unusual. There's not a single person outside. The heat is too intense, the pavement black and burning.

Ben pulls to the curb. The building is gray and squat, with five garage doors in a row. There's no sign, and the front window is scratched with graffiti, the glass foggy and gray.

Ben plucks the piece of paper from your hand, checking the numbers you've written with the numbers on the front of the building. It's the place.

"You shouldn't park here. Keep going—past that tree." You point straight ahead, to where a few bushes and trees block the view from the office. The car rolls forward, then

Ben throws it in park. He's reaching for the door handle when you grab his wrist.

"Wait here for me," you say. "It'll be easier if there's only one of us."

"Are you sure?"

"Please, Ben. You're already in this too deep." You get out of the car and walk away, hoping he won't follow you in.

You keep your head down as you approach the building from the side, aware of the front window, knowing that they can't see you. There's a security camera on one corner of the roof but it points down and away, toward the front door. You don't bother with the office. Instead you circle around back.

There's a man moving boxes off a truck. He spots you just as you turn the corner, and he immediately drops the crate he's holding, coming toward you in a few quick steps. He's not much taller than you. He's covered neck to wrist in tattoos. You look to his waist, his hip, but as far as you can see he's unarmed.

You glance down, pretending to read off the paper. "I was looking for Parillo Construction. Is this it? My cousin told me about you guys and I need someone to repair my—"

"We're not taking on any new jobs."

The man takes another step, blocking you off. Behind him you can see the first garage door is open six inches. It's not locked.

The crates beside the truck are taped shut. You can't make

out any writing on the side and he keeps watching, waiting for you to leave. "I'm sorry, this isn't Parillo? Do you do construction?"

"This used to be Parillo Construction, but it's not anymore."

"But you guys are still listed online—"

"Look. We're closed; now will you let me finish what I'm doing?"

You try to take in as much as possible: the white truck filled with wooden boxes, the back brace you can see through his T-shirt, the barbed wire tattoo that wraps up his left bicep, disappearing beneath his sleeve. Nothing about him is familiar. Still, you take one more look at the garage door behind him. There's something he doesn't want you to see.

After you leave, he follows you out to the edge of the building, watching you cross the street. You ignore Ben in the Jeep, pretending you parked and walked here from a few streets away. You disappear behind a corner.

You go up two blocks, hang a right, then another to circle around. It takes you a few minutes to find a good view of the back lot. The truck is still parked there, the cartons stacked on the pavement. The man is now talking to a woman who's much taller than him, her plum-red hair slicked into a bun. He keeps pointing to the open garage door, then to the front, and you can only hear a few words: *Girl. Parillo. Asking questions.*

The woman says something too low to hear, then the man locks up the truck. They both disappear around the front of the building.

The garage can't be more than thirty feet away—just a sprint across the parking lot. There's only one security camera in the back. You hop the wooden fence and you're gone.

As you approach the door you can hear movement beyond it, though when you press your ear to it, you can't decipher what it is. You pull the handle and light floods the cement room, revealing half a dozen pit bulls, all in their own separate cages. When you open the door they spring to their feet, darting along the periphery of the metal pens, jowls curled back, teeth bared. The barking is so loud your muscles tense up, the shrillness a knife in your ear.

Their faces are scarred. One dog's cheek is ripped away. Another has marks on its front legs, the skin bloody and raw. You push through a door beside them and the stench is so strong it steals your breath. You grab the edge of your shirt, using it to cover your nose.

In the center of that room is a metal ring, the floor stained brown. Folding chairs are set up along the walls. Scanning the corners, you notice the far-left side of the garage, where someone has dug up the concrete. There's a large garbage bag slung into the hole. A few barrels stand beside it.

You approach the bag and kneel down, the smell so strong you can't breathe. You rip a section of the plastic, just below the top, and it's enough to make out the man's chin. His skin is a waxy, bluish-white.

You pull the rest of the plastic away, exposing Ivan's face. His skin looks strangely thin, as if it might slip away from the bone. His eyes are sunken in. His chin is set at a strange angle, the bruises on his cheek still visible, the blood dried black.

You let go of the plastic and step back. The fine hairs on your arms prickle. Your stomach tenses, the rotting stench so strong bile rises up in the back of your throat. You choke it down, your shirt to your face as you leave through the other room, the dogs still barking as you sprint from the building.

CHAPTER TWENTY-SIX

YOU BANG YOUR hand on the dashboard of the Jeep as Ben takes off. You peer out the rear window for any sign of the man or woman behind you.

"Take a right up here," you say. "They might come after us."

"What the hell happened?" Ben asks as he speeds ahead, barely pausing for stop signs.

"They were hiding some dogfighting ring. And . . ."

"And . . . ?"

Ben takes a hard left toward the freeway. As soon as he sees the sign he pulls onto the ramp, barely looking at the direction you're headed.

"And I found a body. Ivan's body. That man who was helping me."

As soon as you say it your throat tightens. You lean

forward, your elbows on your knees, trying to slow your breaths. You knew something bad had happened, somehow you knew, and yet seeing him, seeing his body, makes it all feel real. *It shouldn't have happened like this,* you think as you watch the cars change lanes, the freeway passing beneath you. The photo is still folded in your pocket. You let your hand rest on your leg, feeling it there beneath the fabric, not wanting to look at it—to look at them. He saved your life. He was trying to help you. He lied to protect you.

Once you think it you can't let it go. It repeats on a horrible loop. *He's dead because of you. . . . He's dead because of you. . . . He's dead because of you. . . .*

Ben pulls off at the next exit. He doesn't say anything as he drives, instead taking the turns a little too wide, stopping a little too short. As you approach his house you duck down in the passenger seat, staying hidden, still afraid the cops might be watching. You wait until the Jeep is in the garage to sit back.

Ben leans in, his hand resting on your shoulder. "It's going to be okay."

"How, though? How?" You can't help the edge in your voice. How is anything okay?

"I don't know," Ben says. "There has to be something you can do with this information, someone you can give it to. The cops, maybe. It proves you were telling the truth. It proves they killed him."

He reaches down and takes your hand, folding his fingers into yours. His thumb runs over your skin, tracing the lines inside your palm. Then he sets it down against his chest. You let him hold it there for a moment, enjoying the warmth of his grip, listening to each breath—a reminder you're still alive.

You know he's right. You have to do something, you have to keep going. You squeeze his hand once before slipping away.

CHAPTER TWENTY-SEVEN

"PAPER OR PLASTIC?" The bagger is an elderly man with knobby, arthritic hands. He holds the quart of milk up over a bag, about to set it inside.

"That's okay. I'll just carry it like this," Celia Alvarez says. She hooks her finger in the handle. Then she walks toward the sliding doors, past rows of orchids and roses, crumpling the receipt and tossing it into the trash outside.

The parking lot is quiet. It's nearly eleven o'clock. As she roots around her uniform pocket for her keys, she thinks again of the video from the interview. How many times had she watched it? Gallagher made fun of her, saying she was obsessed, that they knew all they needed to know. Junkies. Arson. They found syringes. They found vodka bottles and gasoline. The girl was at best mentally ill, schizophrenic maybe, suffering some strange hallucinations. She was convinced people were hunting her.

Celia hits the button on her keys, momentarily missing her Civic, which is hidden behind a red van. The taillights glow and there's a beep. She continues toward it. What about the girl's story, though? So much of it matched up. The time line, for one, and her details were internally consistent, her account unwavering. Gallagher said she might've been on drugs. She wasn't, though. There's no way. . . .

Then there was Celia's own story—the one she'd told the two officers as they came around the back of the house, looking for the girl. She'd grabbed the girl's wrist. She'd taken out the handcuffs, but had she really meant to arrest her? When had she ever let someone get away? She only pursued her for a few yards before stopping. She hadn't even climbed the fence.

It was like she was going through the procedure, arresting the girl because she was told to, all the while knowing it wasn't right. It was against her instincts. Had that been it? Had she *wanted* her to get away?

In the past few days Celia found herself looking for the girl as she passed local high schools, wondering if she was walking in those sidewalk crowds. She studied every face of every girl along Hollywood Boulevard. The ones who slept with blankets pulled up to their necks. The ones who sat with cardboard signs. The ones who stood in darkened doorways, asking for a ride.

For this reason she wonders if she's imagining it when she sees the girl sitting beside the red van. The girl stands, backs away, watching Celia's hands to see if she'll reach for the gun. She doesn't. She just takes the girl in. Her black hair falls past her shoulders. Her clothes are clean, though they're several sizes too big, the basketball shorts folded over her hips.

"Please don't do anything," the girl says. "Please just listen. Please."

Celia doesn't need her to beg. She already has this strange motherly instinct to hug her, even though Celia's only thirty-four, with no kids of her own. The girl seems smaller next to the van. Her tone is even but her expression is tentative, as if she's nervous. Afraid?

"I followed you from the police station. You need to know I wasn't lying the other day. All of it. It was all the truth."

"I know," is all Celia can manage.

The girl stands by the van's bumper, watching her, keeping a good ten feet between them. "There was one thing I didn't say at the station," she says. "I only remembered it after. The supplies in the house—they had the name Parillo Construction on the sides. I can't tell whether it's a real company or not, but I went there. I found the body of the man they took, Ivan. Someone was in the process of burying it."

Celia pulls the pad from her front pocket and writes it down. "When was this? Today?"

"This afternoon. There were all these dogs in cages, too. . . . It looked like they were running a dogfighting ring."

"Did they see you?"

"Two people saw me looking around, but they didn't see me go into the garage. They probably haven't moved the body yet."

Celia nods, considering it. She'll have to get a lead on the dogfighting ring, follow it there. She can't let anyone know she saw the girl, that she let her get away again. No one can know this happened.

"One more thing," the girl adds, taking a few steps back. "You said that stuff about San Francisco . . . Club Xenith . . . but there's nothing in the articles about me. Did you find my name or where I'm from? Anything about who I was before?"

Celia leans on her car. The girl's not lying—that's even more obvious now. She really doesn't remember anything before the subway station. She doesn't even know her own name.

"They didn't have a name on file for you," she says. "Everything I've read just has basic info. In San Francisco the other kids called you Trinie. One of them told police you were originally from a town near Palm Springs . . . Cabazon, I think it was."

"Where is that?"

"A couple hours east. It's hard to know whether that's the truth. You were camping in a park in San Francisco. It seemed like most people you were with were runaways. There didn't seem to be a whole lot of information about you."

As Celia says it, she wonders if she should tell her the other piece, the one that she's been thinking about herself. One of the kids is still in juvenile hall outside the Bay Area. A boy who was living there at the same time. She's thought of going there to speak to him. It might not be anything, though. And it's not the type of thing she wants the girl exploring on her own. It's probably too risky to share.

When she looks up the girl is backing away from her, setting out across the empty lot. "Let me drive you somewhere," Celia says. "It's late."

"I'll be okay," the girl says. "The tracking device is gone; they haven't been able to find me for a few days. Please just go there. Please just find him."

"I will, I promise." Celia opens the car door, setting the milk down on the passenger side. She doesn't get in. Instead she watches the girl circle around the back of the store, disappearing through a neighboring yard.

CHAPTER TWENTY-EIGHT

"DUDE, HOW ARE you not bored? I'm getting Pool ADD," Izzy says, pulling her iPhone from her sweatshirt. She turns onto her stomach, then turns back, punching at the screen.

"It's only been an hour." You know because you've been keeping track. An hour since Izzy came over, another two until Ben's back from school, then another three until you'll be getting to Cabazon—the town Celia, the cop, told you about last night. When Izzy knocked on the pool house this afternoon you tried to seem light, breezy even, excusing the last few days away (you were back at your parents', you told her). But it's hard to make conversation now, hard to seem normal.

Izzy points the phone at the vines that have grown over the top of the fence, zooming in on a hummingbird hovering there. She takes video for a few seconds, then sits up, pulling a T-shirt on over her bathing suit.

"I need to do something," she says. "Let's walk to those shops on Hillhurst."

"I'm supposed to wait here until Ben gets back." As soon as you say it you know how it sounds—like you're some pathetic girl who lives for her boyfriend. There's no way to explain to Izzy what's been going on. Last night you and Ben made a plan. You'd go to Cabazon for a couple days and see if you could find anything. If you did grow up there, something about it might trigger your memory.

Izzy smirks. "Okay . . . Sunny Stockholm Syndrome."

"What does that even mean?"

"Stop acting like some brainwashed hostage! I don't want to lie around another day—I'm turning into a banana slug. Come on, we'll be back within an hour."

She steps into her jean shorts and pulls them up, then tosses you your pants and T-shirt, which are piled on the lounge chair. You get up, knowing there's no convincing her. You'll just have to be quick. You'll have to be careful.

By the time you've dressed, Izzy is already out the gate. You follow her down Franklin, the traffic moving beside you. You're wearing the sunglasses Ben lent you, your hair down and obscuring your face, but you can't help but turn back, glancing over your shoulder every now and then.

Izzy walks beside you, stopping for a second to take a picture of a heart-shaped crack in the sidewalk. "So," she says, tucking her phone back into her pocket, "are you going to tell me what's going on?"

"What's going on?"

"You've been zoned out all day. Something happened . . . I just want to know what. Hot, steamy night?" Izzy reaches for your hair but you pull away, your hand jumping to the scar.

"Izzy . . . stop."

"I was just going to check for hickeys."

"Ben's just a friend."

"I have friends like that, too. . . ." Izzy laughs.

Her question brings back a rush from the night before, and you're worried your face will betray you. You fell asleep on the couch beside him, his arm underneath your head, the other wrapped around your waist. As much as you know you shouldn't, you can feel yourself getting attached to him. The house felt empty today without him there.

You pass a street lined with palm trees, their tops towering high above. Row after row of condominiums. A woman on a balcony is smoking a cigarette, her feet crossed over the stone ledge.

Up ahead you notice the street sign—VERMONT. The subway station you woke up in is just south of here, and it's another reminder of how you've lied to Izzy. How can you possibly explain who Ben is? How could she possibly understand?

"It's just . . . complicated," you say.

"It always is. Start from the beginning. Where'd you guys meet?"

"I ran into him at the supermarket. Literally . . . we bumped into each other."

As Izzy walks she holds up her phone, filming the back of the cars as they drive past. "How long ago was that?"

You can't tell her the truth. You've known Ben for a week, and you're staying in his house. "About a year ago. I used to go to his school. Then we moved to the other side of town. Things with my mom got messed up, so I'm looking for a place to stay more permanently."

"Where's your dad?"

You think of the memory from the church, the coffin covered in white cloth. "He died a while ago."

Izzy stops on the sidewalk. She studies you, her head tilted to the side. "I thought your parents have been fighting a lot?"

You take a thin breath, not looking at her. Thankfully a few stores come into view ahead. There's a 7-Eleven across the street, a children's clothing boutique to your right. A woman stands on the corner near some health-food place, her smile oppressively cheerful. "Free smoothie?" she asks. "Promotion runs all week!"

She offers you each a coupon. Izzy studies it, then slips it into the pocket of her sweatshirt. You're hoping the distraction will be enough to draw her out of the conversation, but she keeps glancing sideways at you, waiting for your response.

"I meant my stepdad. He's been with my mom for a while. It's not that interesting. . . ."

"It's not that interesting? Or you don't want to talk about it?" Izzy shakes her head, sending the tuft of black hair away from her face. The piercing in her cheek catches the light.

There's no chance of getting anything past her. You like that about her, but another part of you wishes she wouldn't ask questions, that whatever friendship you're forming can remain on the surface of things.

You follow her down the street, passing the diner you met Ben at, then continuing on toward some clothing stores. A few moments go by before you remember her question. You haven't answered her. Isn't that answer enough?

"I guess I don't want to talk about it," you say.

"I'm starting to think there are the people who like to deal with things head-on and talk them out until they can't talk anymore, and then there are the people who don't say anything and just wish it all away," Izzy says. "I've always been the first kind. I can't be any other way, even if I wanted to."

"Maybe I'm the second," you say. "I'm not sure."

"But don't all those feelings eat you alive? How is your brain not attacking itself? I just don't understand how you people exist."

"'You people'? You make it sound like I'm some kind of monster."

"You are. It's not healthy." Izzy laughs. "And I'm not going to psychoanalyze you and stuff, but whatever you're going through right now, you probably should talk to someone about it. What happened to me at school? That wasn't even my fault, and still, every night me and Mims sit down and try to sort through it."

"You talk about it like it's a choice," you say. "Like you either deal with it or you don't." You can barely think about what happened to Ivan, let alone say it to someone else.

"Isn't everything a choice?"

She doesn't ask you directly. Instead the question is flung into the air, and in that way the conversation doesn't seem as threatening. You head down Hillhurst, two steps behind Izzy, thinking about it—how what she's said is wrong. Not everything is a choice. Some things choose you.

The light at the intersection is red. You pull your hair around the sides of your face, hiding your profile. You scan the sidewalk out of habit, watching two men across the street. They're in medical scrubs, one carrying a manila folder. The way they talk seems so casual, so unaffected, it's almost comforting.

"Look, Scientologists," Izzy whispers, pointing to two women standing in the doorway of a short gray building. A man sits in front of a sign that says FREE STRESS TEST. He gestures to the folding chair across from him.

"Free stress test?" he asks.

You're about to walk away when Izzy steps toward him, studying the small table of books set out under the awning. She picks one up, asking something about aliens.

"We should go," you say, noticing the outdoor café directly across the street. There are sixty or more people there. They have a perfect view of you. You look to the opposite corner, trying to gauge the best way to leave.

"You have to check this out, seriously. . . ." Izzy picks up another book and turns it over, pointing to the erupting volcano on the cover.

Izzy says something else, talking to the man, but you're not listening. Something's off. You can feel it, that strange sensation you're being watched.

You look down the street, and your eyes lock. This time there's no hat, no sunglasses. He looks like any other runner in a simple T-shirt and shorts, gray sneakers. But it's the same man who followed you from the park. Pale, angular face. You can't see the gun but you know it's there.

"I have to go. . . ." you say, starting down the street. In just a few steps you've broken into a run. You don't look back as Izzy calls after you.

You sprint across the street, not waiting for the light to change. Someone leans on their horn. Another car screeches to a stop. You keep going, taking in long, slow sips of air. You want to believe he won't kill you here, that he can't, there's too many witnesses. But as he picks up the pace fear rips through you. No matter how fast you run he's still there.

The intersection south feeds five different roads. You make a quick decision, turning right behind a few sprawling parking lots. Within a block you're in a neighborhood. Small, squat apartment buildings line the road. When you turn back the man is gone. He took a different turn . . . but how long until he finds you?

You move along the edge of the buildings, starting up the sidewalk, where the trees and brush are thicker, providing more cover. Not a single person is outside. There's a busier intersection just a block north. In the sudden shade you feel calmer, more clearheaded. You just have to make it to the corner.

As you pass another apartment complex you're uneasy. You turn, catching sight of him. He's hiding on the second flight of stairs. His forearm rests on the metal balcony, the gun aimed at your head. He fires once, the bullet coming so close you feel the air change in front of you. It buries itself in a nearby car.

The car windshield shatters. The alarm screeches. You break into a sprint but he is already coming down the stairs. You hear his steps on the concrete, the quick rhythm of them as he runs, skipping some, landing hard on the ground.

Just make it to the corner, you think. *You're almost there.* It's so close but there isn't enough space between you. You hear him coming from behind. In just seconds he knocks you down, your palms skidding across the sidewalk. You're on your side, hidden behind a hedge.

You flip onto your back, pulling your legs to your chest. He looks down at you, reaching for the weapon at his waist, and you use that half second to kick as hard as you can with both legs. The blow lands just below his stomach. He folds forward, a wheezing sound escaping his lips.

You get to your feet, sprinting the next few yards to the corner. When you turn back, looking at him one last time, he's bent on the sidewalk, his hand still on his side. The gun fell when you kicked him. He grabs for it but you're already on the main street, a few cars speeding past. A service lets out of a nearby church. People linger by the front doors.

Your eyes meet his. You notice the strange, crooked scar that cuts down the front of his chin, his deep-set blue eyes. You realize, in a flash, that you recognize him . . . you know him.

A yellow taxi comes speeding down the street and without a second thought you jump in front of it, palms outstretched. The driver slams on his brakes, swearing and honking his horn. It's enough to draw everyone's attention. The crowd on the steps of the church is staring at you now. When you look across the street, the man has pocketed his gun.

You open the taxi door, jump into the backseat, and offer to pay any price for the driver to take you back home.

CHAPTER TWENTY-NINE

THE DOCTOR SEES a black sedan approaching, but it's hard to make out the license plates in the rain. They said to look for AX9. A few cars pass, and as he reaches the end of the crosswalk he raises his arm to hail it.

It's coming down harder now, hitting his face, stinging his eyes. He holds up his hand, waiting as the sedan comes closer. He is only a few blocks from the West Side Highway and the streets are quiet except for the cars, speeding along, ripping into puddles, sending dirty water splashing over the curb. A woman stands under the awning of an apartment building, her umbrella flipped inside out. A few other people run back toward the subway station.

As the sedan slows he can make out the plates. AX9. The first few digits are the same. There's a sheet of paper behind the windshield, some sort of fake gypsy cab license, but it's a new guy.

The driver rolls down the window. He's older, with wiry gray hair. He wears a black polo shirt, a gold cross visible under the collar.

"Where to?" he asks.

It always takes the doctor a few seconds. He always thinks before he speaks, knowing he has to get the exact wording right. They're clear about that whenever they contact him. Everything has to be as they specify.

"I'm trying to get downtown. How much to go to Broadway and Spring?"

The driver tilts his head, looking out into the rain. The wipers are going their fastest speed, whipping back and forth, a steady beat.

"How 'bout forty?"

The doctor will say thirty-five, the man will agree, and he will get in the backseat. That is how it will happen, but now that he's here, standing beside the car, he has a moment of hesitation. What has he done? Is Cal unhappy with him?

"Thirty-five?" the doctor asks.

The driver nods. He puts his thumb over his shoulder to say, *Get in.*

The doctor takes one last look out into the rain, scanning the few people on the street. It's not a choice. He has to meet him, he has to do this, but there's still that itch to turn around, head back to the hospital, get his car and just go. Leave. How long would it take them to find him?

He opens the door, slides into the backseat. Cal is there, wearing a crisp black suit and tie. "Richard," he says. "Thanks for meeting me on short notice."

"Of course."

The sedan starts forward and the doctor falls against the seat. His clothes are soaked through. He pushes his hair off his forehead, wiping the rain from his cheeks. He tries not to seem nervous, instead looking out the windshield as the car turns south on Broadway.

"The drug," Cal starts. "You said you were certain about its effectiveness."

Richard shakes his head. "I said I was as certain as I could be. It's all still very experimental. I was clear about that from the beginning."

"You said that in high dosages, the memories wouldn't return for six months, maybe a year. Did you not say that?"

"It was a theory, a working theory. Why? What happened?"

Cal peers out from behind thin wireless glasses. "We're hearing that that's not the case. That there are memories coming through. One of our people was recognized from the island."

The doctor's first impulse is to apologize or explain, and he has to remind himself that he's done nothing wrong. The drug was always experimental. They knew that. He was clear. It had only been used in a handful of studies, mostly PTSD patients, and his theory was just that—a theory. When they'd tested the high dosage it had worked, for only three weeks, but it had worked.

"I saw it work," he insists. "You saw it work."

"It's not working anymore. It's been less than a month and the memories seem to be coming back for some of them."

"It was always experimental. You asked me to suppress years. Their time on the island, something that big . . . It was never certain."

Cal fiddles with his cuff link. When he says it his voice is even, and it's a statement, not a question. He never asks. "We'll need more."

The doctor lets out a breath. He watches the city go by beyond the window, trying to think of how to say it. He can't just get more of the drug, but they have to think he can. Cal needs to need him.

"You'll have to give me time," he says.

"We don't have any."

"You can't just expect me to get it for you in a day. I'll need two weeks . . . at least."

"One."

Cal signals to the driver, and the sedan pulls to the curb. They haven't reached Broadway and Spring. Instead they've stopped above Union Square. The Flatiron Building is a block south.

"I'll try."

"Do better than try," Cal says. "Or you may end up on the island yourself."

Then he reaches over the doctor, opens the door, and gestures for him to get out. The rain is coming down harder now. The drains are flooded, water rising up to the curb. The doctor wants to say something to convince him, to get him on his side, but Cal stares straight ahead. He is waiting for him to leave.

The doctor steps out. He is soaked again, the rain so hard it stings when it hits his skin. He closes the door and the car pulls away.

For a few moments he just stands there, unable to move. He thinks of the men he'd treated from the island, the ones who'd come back with their arms ripped open, flesh rotted from infection. One had a five-inch spearhead driven into his back, just to the right of his spine. The doctor examined the bloody shard. Tiny barbs had been carved into the tip to make it impossible to pull out.

The doctor takes a long, thin breath, letting his heart slow. Cal and his fucking threats. It's still in his head as the car takes a right down Twenty-First Street, disappearing from view.

CHAPTER THIRTY

"HOW DO THEY feel?" Ben asks, glancing at your hands.

You're looking down at your pink, scraped palms, the bruising just starting to darken. The skin burns where it hit the pavement. "They're fine," you say. "And I'm fine . . . better, at least. I'm just relieved we're away from LA."

By the time the taxi dropped you off, Ben was already home. You told him what happened with the hunter, and he ushered you into the Jeep before taking off for Cabazon. The more miles you put between you and Los Angeles, the more you could relax, the shaking in your hands subsiding. Three hours later, there's no sign of anyone following you. You have to hope he can't get to you here.

Ben turns the Jeep down a main strip, past another row of houses. Cabazon is a desert town, the orange sand stretching to the mountains, the buildings faded by the sun. Just off the freeway there's a gas station with two giant dinosaur sculptures outside. As Ben parked, refilling the tank, you studied them, wondering how many times you'd passed them before today. How long had you lived here? Did you grow up nearby? Is there someone waiting for you to come back?

"I just need to know something, anything," you say, scanning the dirt road. The houses are set far back, beyond sand and dry brush, tiny rectangular structures bleached by the sun. Nothing about this place seems familiar. "I feel like I'm running out of time."

Your voice is uneven and you turn away, hoping Ben doesn't see the sudden swell in your eyes. "Don't talk like that," he says. "You got away from him twice. You're strong and smart and from now on I'll be there with you, wherever you go. Whatever you need. That police officer, she's putting the pieces together. She's going to find them."

Ben brakes at the stop sign and a woman crosses in front with two small boys, both riding bicycles, the training wheels still on. You didn't wear your glasses, and now you meet the woman's gaze through the windshield, watching her cross. For once you *want* someone to recognize you. You're hoping she'll smile, you're hoping she'll wave.

But they just keep moving. She says something to the boys, resting her hand on the littler one's back. Ben takes another turn, circling another block, and you pass a birthday party in someone's yard. Colorful paper flags are strung up in decoration. There's music playing. "How does someone go from living here, having some normal life, to what I've been through? How does that even happen?"

Ben doesn't respond. He just puts his hand on your arm as he takes another turn, moving back toward the town center. The main area can't be more than ten square miles, and in the last hour he's driven up and down the streets, past parks and playgrounds, schools and libraries and supermarkets. How many drugstores have you seen? How many restaurants? You keep studying the faces of strangers, wondering if you knew them before.

The sun is going down, the sky deepening to pinks and golds. You pass a shopping complex, some advertisements on the wall beside it. You're drawn to one particular one. It pictures a blond woman in a white sequined gown, LULA'S BRIDAL written underneath it in big, loopy script. The woman has a bright purple flower tucked behind one ear. It's faded, the ad ripped in places, but it's familiar. The memory rushes in.

The yellow paint on the house is peeling. You stick your finger beneath it, ripping it off, watching how the chips break apart in your hand. You're younger, you can sense that, and before you can turn away a little boy runs up to you. He has black hair and black eyes and a handful of sand. He throws it to your back.

"Gotcha!" Then he is off, cutting into the yard.

You run after him. He can't be more than five years old but he is fast. He jumps some tires sitting in the sand, tears around a broken television set that was thrown beside the barbed-wire fence. He starts into the front yard. Down the road, high above a few dingy houses, is a billboard for a place called Lula's Bridal. The bride wears bright purple eye shadow, her hair teased out three inches.

The boy circles again, back around the other side of the house, slipping through a gap in the wire fence. You follow, hopping over a rusted ladder. It's your house, that's clear. You know every stepping-stone, know where the dog has dug ditches, know about the wooden boards tucked behind the side door.

You are running and you are happy, laughing, and so is he. He turns back and his eyes catch the light. His smile is all teeth and in an instant you can feel it: You love this place and you love him. You cut around the house, running to him then, your little brother.

———

"It felt so real," you repeat. "He was right there. It was like I was with him again."

After you came out of the memory, Ben drove around, trying to find the yellow house, but nothing turned up. It must have been painted in the years since, and the bridal store must have closed. No one you asked had heard of it, and the billboard you saw in the memory has since been taken down. The peeling advertisement from the town center is the only indication the store was ever there.

"When you had that other memory, it felt the same way?" Ben pulls into the convenience-store parking lot. The fluorescent light streams through the front window, casting a strange glow on his face.

"It was that vivid, yeah."

"What was it of?"

"I could see this church, this funeral. I didn't know who it was for, though. Just that I was reading something at it."

"It's coming back, then," he says. "Your memory is going to come back."

He rests his hand on the door handle, kissing you once before he takes off into the store, having promised a 7-Eleven dinner.

You pull your notepad from the glove compartment, writing down a few lines:

- House was originally yellow
- Located by the freeway, near a billboard
- Lula's Bridal
- Brother was younger, with dark hair and eyes

You're still looking at the notes when there is a knock on the window. The man must be in his forties, with greasy gray hair that sticks up in all directions. He has a large, bulbous nose, covered in thin red veins. His eyes are glazed over. You move your hand to the door, trying to push the lock down without being too obvious.

But he smacks the door with his hand. "Awwww, now

you're driving around in some fancy car and actin' like you don't know me. I see what happened. And here I was, I was being a kind, good-hearted person, I said, *Shorty Do! You gotta help her! You know she always needs someone to buy it for her!*"

You watch him through the window. He gestures with his hands, occasionally slapping his leg for emphasis. Does he actually know you?

"What do you mean? Buy what?"

The man leans in and winks. "Yeah, 'what' is right. I won't tell."

"I was being serious. . . ."

"You still like the big bottle of Wild Turkey, eh? I'll get it for you, but then you gotta give me a little of it. I don't need to take much today, just a little."

You roll down the window, wondering if it's possible he does recognize you. "We know each other? From when?"

"You're messing with me?"

"No, I'm not. . . . I just don't remember. I can't remember a lot of things now. Something happened."

The man glances inside the store, turns back to you. "You look kind of different . . . but I knew it was you. I haven't seen you in, I don't know, a year? Who's that boy?"

"What's my name?"

"How would I know? You used to come up to me, asking me to help you, and then one day those men were talking to you. You just up and left with them. I never saw you till now."

"What did they look like?"

He puts his hands in his filthy jeans, pushing them deeper into his pockets. Then he nods into the car, at the center console. There's five bucks sitting in an old coffee cup. "Help me out?"

You can see Ben inside the store, the back of his head just visible over the candy aisle. You pluck it from the cup and pass it to him. "Who were they? What did they look like?"

"I don't remember. Fancy lookin'! I didn't see 'em before that day."

"I knew them?"

"Knew 'em, you were waiting for them."

It's hard to imagine. You wanted him to say they took you, that you left fighting, screaming. That it wasn't your choice.

"Did you ever see me with anyone else, besides them?"

"Some kid. Little younger than you."

You look down at the notebook, at the description of your brother. Your lungs feel tight. "What did he look like? What was his name?"

"He looked kind of like you, black hair, pretty brown eyes. I don't know. . . ."

You write everything he says, trying to ignore that he's called you pretty. "What else? How many times did I ask you to do that? Do you know where I lived?"

He laughs, backing away from the car window. He's watching the road behind you, the passing traffic. He checks the corners of the building, for what, you're not sure. Something must've scared him.

You turn around, noticing the security guard on the other side of the parking lot. The guard yells something you can't quite make out. He gestures with his hand for the guy to leave you alone.

"I only saw you a few times," the man says as he starts away. "That's all I know."

As he cuts across the lot Ben comes out of the store carrying two bags. He watches the man approaching a woman on the curb, then looks back at you. "What is it? What's wrong?"

"That guy . . . he thinks he knows me," you say. "He said I used to come here asking him to buy me alcohol. He saw me over a year ago—I left with two men. He said I was with a younger boy sometimes. I think it was my little brother."

Ben slides into the car. Together you sit and watch the man. He's waving his arms as he speaks, his hair falling into his face. He yells something at the woman that you can't hear. She has a metal cart filled with old blankets.

"What else did he say?"

"That's all. I tried to ask him more but he looked at me like I was crazy."

Ben stares out the window. "Let me get this straight . . . *he* looked at *you* like *you* were crazy?"

You turn, seeing what he sees. The man has pulled his shirt up, his belly sticking out, a thick strip of underwear showing in the back. He smacks his ribs a few times and yells something that sounds like "Jell-O jigglers!"

"I see your point."

Ben grabs your hand and squeezes. "So it was real, then, just like you said. They must've found you here. You have a brother; you lived close by. What that cop said was right."

"Yeah . . . but where? When?"

You look down at the notebook, writing a description of the man, and the exact address of the convenience store in case you need to find him again. It's hard to know if you believe him, but the pieces fit together. You lived here. This is where they found you. You have a little brother. You wonder where he is now, if he's looking for you.

As Ben pulls out of the parking lot you watch the man, raising your hand in good-bye.

CHAPTER THIRTY-ONE

IT'S ALMOST TEN o'clock when Ben comes back to the motel room. You're sitting on the balcony overlooking the pool, the dinner of packaged sandwiches and pita chips spread out on the table. You've poured the bottle of Coke into two of the motel glasses.

He looks at the two queen beds beside each other, his lips curling into a smile. "Good thing we got the two beds. I was worried you were going to try to take advantage of me."

"You've foiled my plans." You laugh. "What did the front-desk guy say? Did he know anything?"

Ben sits down across from you, takes a swig of the soda. "He said that bridal store closed five years ago at least. It must have been an old ad that we saw."

"So there's no way to find the house, then," you say. "The billboard doesn't even exist."

"Not anymore . . ."

"So I *probably* have a younger brother. . . . So I *might've* bought alcohol from that guy. So they *probably* found me here, whoever *they* are. Where does that leave me?"

You don't look at Ben as you speak, instead staring out over the tiny kidney-shaped pool. Most of the lounge chairs are broken. One of the outside walls has been patched with duct tape. The hallways smell of cigarette smoke; the carpets are dirty. It feels like there's less possibility in it now—this town, this place.

"Maybe more memories will come back. Maybe it's just a matter of time."

"Maybe . . ." you say, but it's hard not to feel discouraged. You saw the house so clearly; it was so vivid. How could you be so close and have no way to find out where it is? How many streets had you driven down tonight, looking for it, just hoping to recognize something? Is your brother still somewhere, searching for you, waiting for you to come back?

"You had to come here," Ben adds. "If you didn't, you would've always wondered."

"So this is all I get? Some passing memory, a nickname that can't be traced? What if this is all I *ever* get?"

"Maybe that's not so bad. . . ."

"What do you mean?"

Ben rests his chin in his hands. He opens his mouth, but for a moment he just looks at you, as if he's puzzling out what to say. "I don't know," he starts. "It's just . . . there are things that I've wanted to forget before. Shitty things, things that it would be easier if I didn't have to think about. And there are people I've wanted to forget. Maybe whatever happened before, however bad things were—maybe this is your chance."

"My chance to be someone else?"

"Yeah," he says. "To be who you want to be."

You think of the lists from the notebook. Every time you return to the things you know about yourself, they seem to lead only one place: You were a runaway. You were in and out of juvenile hall. You know how to do bad things, how to hurt people. The boy, the one from the dreams, is the only person who seems to have cared about you, and you're not even certain he's real.

"Your chance for a fresh start." Ben looks down when he says it, his voice quieter than before. "I guess that's kind of what you've been for me. Everything feels different now, new. I mean, after my dad died and everything happened with my mom, I sort of felt trapped, stuck. It was like nothing mattered, nothing I could do would change anything, you know? But now . . . meeting you . . . seeing the way you've handled everything . . . I feel better. Like maybe I don't have to sit around accepting what's happened. Maybe I can make things the way I want, be the person I want to be."

You meet his eyes and you both smile. Your cheeks feel hot. Before you can think or question, you stand, stepping toward him, closing the space between you, your knees just inches from his. You grab his hand, your fingers folding together. "Are you saying you like me, Ben?"

He lets his head fall back, looking up at you, and there is that smile again—bright, blinding. "I guess, yeah. I do."

He stands, moving toward you, and within a few steps you are against the wall. You let his hand wander to the back of your head. It traces along your jaw, his fingers brushing your chin. His other hand is still holding on to yours. He tightens his grip as he leans down, his mouth against your mouth, pushing your head back.

Everywhere you go he is there. He is holding you against him, his lips moving to your cheeks, touching down on your eyelids. He pauses, pulling your collar over to kiss your shoulder, just once.

You let your fingers sweep up his back, skimming under his shirt, where his skin is soft and smooth. He moves both hands to your hips, picking you up in one swift motion. He turns around, spinning you inside the cool motel room, setting you down on one of the queen beds.

You lie back, watching as he peels off his shirt. He's tall and thin, all ropy muscle, his skin still tan and freckled from the summer. He sets a hand on either side of your head, lowering himself on top of you, kissing you again.

"I thought you wanted your own bed," you say.

He laughs, his breath in your hair. When your eyes meet

his you can see every fleck of blue and gray in the irises. "I changed my mind."

"Are you sure? I wouldn't want to take advantage of you. . . ."

He reaches down around your waist, tugging your shirt up and over your head, urging off your sports bra, his fingers reaching to the waist of your pants. "I think I'll be okay," he says.

You keep whispering to him, questioning it . . . "Are you okay?" . . . "What about now?" . . . as his mouth moves to your ear. One hand is on your ribs, sliding up, kneading your breast.

"I'm okay, I'm more than okay. . . ." he repeats. Then he smiles, burying his face in your neck.

———

You're half asleep, comforted by the feeling of Ben tracing a line across your shoulder blades, his finger running down your spine, over each vertebrae, circling one, then the next. You pull the blankets to you. Your eyes are closed. You listen to the rhythm of his breaths, how they slow, then change, pausing as if he wants to say something.

"We could go somewhere," he finally says, his voice barely a whisper. "It might be better for you out of the city."

"What do you mean?"

"We could start over. Whatever we've done . . . whoever we were . . . or weren't . . . it won't matter."

"Fresh start?" You turn over, staring up at the ceiling. He's watching the side of your face, waiting. He smiles.

"Yeah," he says. "Maybe for a while. It'll be safer."

You look at him, feeling for his hand under the covers, pulling it up beside your heart. You move closer, letting your forehead rest against his chest. His breath comforts you as you close your eyes. "A fresh start . . ."

CHAPTER THIRTY-TWO

YOUR BACK IS on the ground. You can feel the rocks and sticks beneath you, one branch jutting into your shoulder, the pain sharp. The man is above you. His chin is cut and the wound spills blood all over his neck. For the first time you see his eyes, small and pale blue, squeezing shut as he lays his hands down on your neck.

Your throat closes off. His fingers dig into your skin and you are holding his wrists but it's no use. You scratch and pull but he keeps pressing down. Every muscle in his arms is visible. The veins rise up beneath his skin. One knee is on either side of your hips. As he pins you against the earth, the blood drips from his chin onto your forehead.

Your eyes close. All the air in your lungs is gone. Your body is empty, a tight, squirming feeling taking over as you open your lips, trying to get just one breath. You feel yourself giving in, your grip weakening.

Suddenly his hands are off you and you are gasping, taking in as much air as you can. Your face is covered in blood. When you look up you see the boy behind him. He holds a thick branch, sharpened at one end, the bark stained black. The man is slumped on top of your legs. The back of his head is bleeding and you can feel the warmth of it soaking through your clothes.

You push back, freeing yourself from underneath him. When you stand you realize your ankle is swollen and twisted. The boy presses his shoulder under your arm and starts to run, carrying you with him. He keeps looking back into the forest.

"We have to go," he says. "They're coming."

You turn, looking where he looks, when you hear the first gun-shot.

———

2:23 A.M. Your heart is alive in your chest. The streetlamp outside the motel filters in through the venetian blinds. Ben is sleeping beside you, his arm still outstretched, his fingers open, searching for yours. You ease yourself off the bed, careful not to wake him.

The man was there, on the island. You knew him from before. When you close your eyes again you can still feel it, the rising panic as he choked you, how the air was trapped in your chest. You can still see the crooked scar that slices down his chin. He has hunted you before.

You pull the notepad from the canvas duffel on the floor. Holding him in your mind, with the dream still so fresh, is enough to tell you what you need to know. You fold back a page and write:

- *The man with the gun tried to kill you before*
- *He hunted you in the forest (the island?)*
- *The boy was there with you. He saved you from the hunter.*

You sit back, staring at the page, taking in all that it implies. You have been hunted by this man before. The three of you existed somewhere else before this. The three of you . . . which means *the boy* is real. Where is he now? Is he still alive?

You copy down the detail about the hunter's scar, the strange angle it cut across his chin. He's still in Los Angeles, waiting for you to return, waiting for another chance.

You can go somewhere with Ben, but you will always be wondering if he'll track you there. Whoever he is, wherever he is, there is no safety if he's alive. You have to find him.

CHAPTER THIRTY-THREE

THE NEIGHBORHOOD COMES into view ahead. You recognize a few houses on the corner, thick bougainvillea covering the facade, another with a stained-glass window in the front. As Ben drove, the freeway signs counting down the miles to Los Angeles, you kept slipping into silence, everything coming back to you. The woman who followed you. The garage where you found Ivan's body. The man with the gun.

As Ben turns into the driveway his iPhone rings, the screen in the center console flashing *Mom*. "Shit, I have to get this. . . ."

He parks, grabs the phone, and steps out of the car, cutting across to the front yard. "Hi, I know, I'm sorry," he immediately says, his voice getting farther away.

You pull the bag from the backseat and circle around the

back of the house, knowing you have to find Celia Alvarez again, to talk to her. There hasn't been any news about that building or Ivan's body being discovered, still no information on the woman who was shot beneath the freeway. You need to know what she knows, what she's found.

There's a chance Ivan has already been replaced, that there is someone else tracking you now, following your movements. How else could the hunter have found you when you were out with Izzy? But there's nothing on you—you've checked every pocket of your pants, the hems of T-shirts, the pages of the notepad.

You find the spare key, and as soon as you're inside the house you go to Ben's computer, pulling up a map. You're jotting down the directions on a paper napkin when Ben finally comes downstairs. "What is this, 1995? We need to get you a smartphone." He laughs.

"Is everything okay? What did she say?"

"I have to go visit today. She left a bunch of messages while we were in Cabazon and I guess she's kind of freaking out. Some teacher called and told her how much school I've missed. I just have to go there and show her everything's fine. I'll be back as soon as I can—just a few hours."

"It's all right. I want to go see that police officer today. She must've turned up something by now."

"You really have to?" Ben asks.

"I can't just sit around waiting for him to come back."

"Promise me you'll be safe."

"I'm always safe . . . as I can be. . . ."

Ben pulls you to him. When he says it he doesn't look at you, instead whispering the words into your neck. "When I get back . . . maybe we could just go."

You turn your head, meeting his eyes. Last night you'd assumed it was just something he was saying, some dream you'd talk about and never actually go through with.

"Ben . . . you were serious? You can't just leave your life."

"What life? What do I have here?"

"School. Friends."

Ben grabs a prescription-pill bottle from the coffee table, holding it up. "Friends? I have people who buy drugs from me. Sometimes they come over and watch the Dodgers game and smoke up. Sometimes I sell them some of my mom's old pills."

"Ben . . ."

He wraps his arms around your shoulders, resting his chin on your head, kissing the top of it. It's so sweet and simple it makes you want to cry.

"I'll be back this afternoon," Ben says. "Just think about it? We have a car, we have money. We can go somewhere they won't be able to find you."

You close your eyes, imagining it. You and Ben on a beach somewhere, the sun blazing above, all of this behind you, a distant memory. You breathe him in, all of him, letting your face press deeper into his shirt. You don't know if it's even possible, if there's anywhere they can't find you. There's only one way out of this, you know that, deep in your gut, but you can't say it aloud. Not to Ben.

"Okay." You nod. "I'll think about it."

CHAPTER THIRTY-FOUR

THE WINDOW IS open, and you can smell the sweet peanut sauce on the Thai food. You watch Celia as she moves around her kitchen, holding the plastic container in one hand as she reads the magazine on the counter. Occasionally she dips her chopsticks into the flat noodles, releasing a small bite into her mouth.

When you knock on the back door she reaches to her waist, her hand on the butt of the gun, before realizing it's you. "I've been hoping you'd find me," she says, opening the door. She immediately locks it behind you. "You're all right?"

"I am for now."

She looks different here, in this small Spanish-style house with lights strung up on the back porch. Her dark hair frames her face. She wears a V-neck T-shirt and jeans, the holster at her hip. "I've been worried about you."

"I've been okay. . . ." you say, knowing that's not really true. But it doesn't matter now. "I need to know: Did you find the body?"

Celia moves around the kitchen, pulling a folder from above one of the slots in her dish rack. There's a yellow pad with messy scrawl all over it. "You were right . . . he was there. They're doing the autopsy tonight. They're trying to keep it from the media right now. It's hard to know what to make of it."

"I told them what to make of it. What more proof do they need? That's Ivan. I told you they took him, and now he's dead."

Celia lets out a deep breath. "I know that, but they don't. It turns out his name wasn't Ivan. It was Alexi Karamov. And he doesn't have any obvious connections to crime, even to that dogfighting ring. We couldn't find a single person who had a problem with him."

"So that's it? Another dead end?" You can't help the edge in your voice. This was supposed to be the thing that proved what you'd told them. The thing that would make them believe you. What now? Where can you possibly go from here?

Celia flips through the pages, her brows drawing together. "I have to ask you something," she says, looking down at the leather wristband Ben lent you. "Can I see your arm?"

Your throat tightens. "Why? What now?"

"You said these people are hunting you, right?" Celia says. "So I looked through John Doe and Jane Doe records, different unsolved homicides across the country. I found two different cases—one in Seattle, one in New York. Two bodies turned up with right hands severed at the wrist. Both of them were teenagers, not much older than you."

"They were kids. . . ."

"Yes. And both had records. People are saying maybe it's gang-related, maybe a serial killer, but I know it isn't. Not after what you told me."

You reach down, pulling the wristband away, showing her the bird on the inside of your wrist. You can barely speak, barely breathe as she runs her fingers over it, studying the numbers there.

She holds up her phone. "Can I take a picture?"

You nod and she snaps a few takes, zooming in on the numbers and letters. You thought it might be your initials, your birthday. You thought it could've been something you chose for yourself, something that held some meaning you didn't yet understand. But deep down you had to have known the truth. It's just a brand. . . . It was always a brand. A way for them to identify you.

You are no one. The thought is there and you can't let it go. *You are no one.*

Celia must see it in your face, because she reaches out, resting her hand on your arm, pulling you to her. "We're going to figure this out," she says. "I promise you. It's going to end soon."

You nod, wanting to believe her. When you step back you press your fingers to your eyes, blotting them. "I came here because I need to know who they are."

"The people who came after you?"

"Exactly . . . did you find anything? There has to be something somewhere about the woman who was hunting me. How can a person just die in the middle of Los Angeles and leave no trace?"

Celia nods, and for the first time, she looks tired. "I know, and I've been looking. I searched every obit and homicide report, but . . ."

"What about missing persons? Someone she's close to might not know what she was involved in. Maybe they reported her."

Celia writes something down on the paper. "I'll check. I'll let you know."

Then she goes to the cabinet above the refrigerator, pulling down a paper bag. "This was the best I could do right now," she says, passing it to you.

You open the top. Inside is another vial of mace, a switchblade knife, and a small silver phone. You take it out, turning it over in your hand.

"It's untraceable," she says. "You can use it for thirty days—calls, texts, whatever. Keep it on you. If I hear anything I'll let you know."

"Thanks," you say.

Celia grabs her keys from the counter. "Let me drive you somewhere."

Your first instinct is to tell her no, you'll be fine, she's done enough. But even in daylight you feel uneasy, as if your time is almost up.

"Just to the bus stop," you say. "I'm heading back east."

CHAPTER THIRTY-FIVE

THE LIGHTS ARE all off at Ben's house. He hasn't gotten back yet. Once you're inside, alone in the quiet, you're not certain what to do. You can shower. You can pack the few things you own, get ready to leave with Ben, hoping they won't find you wherever you go next. Is that really an option?

You cut out the back door, approaching the pool house. A pink sticky note is attached to the front window. *WTF? —I* is written in loopy script.

Izzy. You close your eyes and you can see her there, her confused expression as you ran from her on the street the other day. What does she think of you now? It shouldn't matter, she's going back to New York, but you still feel responsible somehow, like it's a wrong you need to right.

You take the spare key Ben gave you and cross into the

next yard. When you get to her porch, you knock, listening to the music that floats behind the door. Mims answers. She has the clearest blue eyes, giving the impression that she's looking through you. Her face is relaxed. She smiles without smiling.

"You must be Sunny," she says. "Izzy told me about you." She puts her hand on your shoulder, leading you inside.

The house is full of light. A stereo is on in the corner, playing some slow music you don't recognize. There's a cutting board out, slices of apples and beets scattered all over it. Mims tosses a handful in the juicer.

"I'm just here to say hi. . . ."

"You're friends with Ben, right? It's nice for her to know a few people here when she visits."

"Yeah." You force a smile, wondering where you'll be when Izzy comes back to LA. If you'll still be around. If you'll still be alive. "Is she here?"

"Inside." Mims points to a hallway off the living room. Her house is smaller than Ben's and sparser. A low coffee table is surrounded by colorful pillows and cushions for people to sit on the floor. In the corner of the room, there are statues on a small altar. Elephants and Buddhas huddle on the bookcase and along the window ledge.

You take the right down the hallway, and as soon as you get to Izzy's door you can smell it—the mixture of pot and incense. You don't bother knocking.

"What the fuck?" She snubs out a joint in the ashtray. "Where did you come from?"

"Sorry about the other day."

Izzy pulls her black hair away from her face, tying the top of it in a knot, exposing the shaved side. She folds her legs into her and just looks at you—this cold, unblinking stare.

"You should be. You ran away from me."

"I got freaked out."

"By what?" Izzy laughs. "It was weird, and I like weird. But that was even too weird for me."

Izzy looks strange here, in this guest room, with a simple white bedspread and a teal blanket slung over the end. The walls are bare. Her clothes and things are piled on the chairs and floor.

"I just wanted to say good-bye."

She doesn't take her eyes off you. She just smacks the end of the bed, telling you to sit down. "I guess you're leaving me in suspense, huh? I know we only spent two days together, but I'm not a total idiot. I know something's going on."

"I can't, Izzy."

"I get it. But you should at least know something before you go. . . ." She pauses. "I saw you."

Your first instinct is the surveillance picture, but then you're confused. Izzy's face doesn't reveal much. She pinches the end of her piercing, turning it around, back and forth between her fingers.

"I don't know what you're talking about."

"I saw you that day by the pool. You were going to steal my wallet."

You take in a breath, but you can't get enough air. You'd give anything to just disappear right now, to close your eyes and be gone, away from this room, out from under Izzy's gaze.

You turn away. "I don't know how to respond. . . ."

"I'm not telling you to make you feel like shit. I'm telling you because you don't seem like the kind of person who would steal unless you really needed it." Izzy reaches over to the nightstand drawer. She pulls a few twenties from her wallet and hands them to you. "It's all I have. Just take it."

"Izzy . . . please don't." It's hard to even look at her. You stare at the floor, at the pile of alcohol bottles peeking out from under her bed, at the crumpled clothes, anywhere but at her. You feel like you are shrinking into yourself.

"It's not a big deal, just take it. You need it, so take it."

Your whole body flushes, the room hotter than before. Out of all the times to run you want to go now, to leave, to never come back. You're looking at your feet when you hear a low binging sound. "What is that?" you ask.

"Not mine," Izzy says. She points to your pocket.

You feel your hip, remembering the cell phone you got from Celia. When you pull it out it has one picture text.

No missing persons fitting the time line but found a report of a car sitting in a lot in Riverside for days. Registered to a female in her early 40s. Husband says she's away on business travel and came to claim the car, but feels strange to me. Here's a pic of the owner—Hilary Goss. Is this the woman who chased you?

You scroll down to the picture, the woman with brown hair and eyes. She is looking at you, her face as clear as it was that day in the alley. Her makeup is done and she's wearing the silver medallion around her neck. You'd recognize her anywhere.

Izzy's still staring at you. "Seriously, since when do you have a phone?"

"I need your computer. . . ." You get up from the bed, fumbling through the clothes on her chair, looking for her laptop.

She pulls it from her nightstand and hands it to you. "Why?"

You flip it open, typing in the name from Celia's text. *Hilary Goss.* You add *Los Angeles*, your hands shaking.

"What the hell is going on? You're scaring me."

You scroll down and for a moment your lungs are tight, the pressure in your chest like nothing you've felt before. There's a *Los Angeles Times* article about a charity auction. You check the caption twice, not wanting to believe it. *Hilary and Henry Goss Host Charity Auction at Their Los Feliz Home.* They're standing in front of their house, her in a summer dress, him in a pressed shirt and tie. They're smiling. You can't stop looking at him. He has the same eyes. The same pale, angular face. The same crooked scar cutting down his chin.

Henry Goss is the man hunting you.

Their street is listed in the story. In minutes you have the route mapped out. Their house can't be more than two miles away, maybe less. You should be able to recognize it from the picture.

"I'm sorry, I have to go." You pass Izzy the computer, trying to stop the trembling in your hands. When you stand to leave she follows you.

"What do you mean? What's wrong?"

Within a few steps you are in the hallway, out beyond the living room, and to the door. It's a pathetic lie but you say it anyway. "Nothing."

You hear her stop at the end of the hall. Her eyes are on your back, as if one simple look can turn you around. You keep going, cutting through the empty living room, the door falling shut behind you.

CHAPTER THIRTY-SIX

THE HOUSE HAS a high metal gate around the perimeter. The surveillance camera points toward the driveway. You stay behind it, moving back along the wall, to where a lemon tree curves over the property.

You climb the trunk of the tree, grabbing on to the awning of leaves above. It curves up, its branches twisting together, making it hard to go much farther. The courtyard below is empty. There aren't any cameras on this side of the house. You press your foot onto the top of the metal rail and push over, hanging down on the other side. It's a fifteen-foot drop. You land hard, a quick pain shooting up your ankle.

The sun reflects off the windows and it's impossible to tell if the lights are on, if anyone is inside. It's a massive Spanish villa, with rough stucco walls and a red clay roof. You circle around back, where a fake waterfall cascades down rocks and into a still pool. You feel for the knife in your pocket.

The back sliding doors are locked. Pressing your face to the glass, you can see the kitchen is empty. The counters are clear. The table doesn't have a single thing on it. Around the side of the house there's another door, this one with a window in the top half. The panes are only six inches by four, one just inside of the doorknob. You grab a rock from a garden a few feet away, aiming it at the thin pane. With one quick jab it breaks, and your hand is inside, turning the lock.

There's no alarm—at least not one that's audible. You're aware that you may only have ten minutes, maybe less, that you should move through as quickly as possible. The house is quiet. To the right of the kitchen is a massive living room. There's a leather sofa, chairs, a zebra-skin rug. Over the fireplace is the mounted head of a spotted cat. You move closer, examining it. It's not until you touch it that you're certain it's real. How long have they been hunting? Where? When did killing animals stop being enough for them?

The stairwell is covered in framed awards. There are several diplomas—business schools and law degrees, professional awards. You climb the twisting staircase to an upper hall. A glass case sits at the end of a long corridor. It's filled with different-size guns, some rifles, some handguns, like the one the woman, Hilary Goss, had with her the day she chased you.

You pass two bedrooms. Both the first and second have nothing in the dressers. The beds are made, the closets empty except for a few old suitcases. You cut across the hall to an office that overlooks the front yard. There are papers stacked on the desk. You sift through them, looking for something to tell you more about the game.

There are bills and contracts, most of which seem to be related to Hilary Goss's business. From what you can tell she worked in finance, the letterhead from a company called Robertson Arthur, some detailing a recent merger. It's all the same, paper after paper. The filing cabinets are all locked. There's a glass award sitting on the windowsill, dated less than two weeks ago, honoring her. HILARY GOSS. RECOGNITION IN OUTSTANDING ACHIEVEMENT, it says.

You move through to the master bedroom. You pull open the dresser drawers, toppling them onto the floor, sifting through shirts and socks. One by one you go down them, but there's nothing inside except clothes. You move through the closets, sweeping aside the hangers. You pick up stacks of sweaters, search under the shelves, slipping your fingers along each ledge to see if there's anything you've missed.

You take another swipe at an upper shelf and your hand stops on a pair of pants. They're folded in a neat square. They don't move. You push at them and tug, but still you can't get them off the shelf. It's not until you lift them up that the lever comes free. They're part of a secret compartment in the top shelf.

You grab an armchair from the corner, moving it to the closet to stand on. From above you can see how the shelf has been hollowed out. The pants are fastened to a thin piece of wood that lifts up. When you move it aside you see the yellow envelope beneath.

You sit down on the floor, handling the envelope as if it's made of glass. There's another folder with a logo on it: A&A Enterprises. You empty the envelope first, the glossy photos spilling onto the floor. It's you. The first one is just of your face, your hair pulled back, your top lip swollen and bloody. You're looking right at the camera, but you don't have any memory of when or where it was taken. The next two are close-ups of your scars—the one on your neck, along with a third crescent-shaped one near your left ankle. The third zooms in on the tattoo on your wrist. All of them are labeled *Blackbird*. All of them have the A&A Enterprises logo on the top.

On the back of the first one is a printed paragraph.

Blackbird: Los Angeles Target
Blackbird has been one of our most elusive targets. She lasted the full fifteen days on the island, making alliances with one other target and injuring two hunters. She is intelligent and cunning. Incredibly fast, she has outrun every hunter who has pursued her. Skills include: tracking, knife skills, and disarming.

You move through the folder, trying to find more information on your background. There's nothing. No explanation of who you were before, no explanation of where you came from. Where was the island? Is the "alliance with one other target" referencing the boy who saved you?

The folder is filled with paperwork. There's not enough time to read it all. You scan through it, noticing a contract between Hilary Goss, Henry Goss, and the company. But it's the letter behind it that raises the fine hairs on your arms. You see the heading from A&A Enterprises. It's made out to Henry only, dated less than a week before. *Due to the nature of your wife's death and your history with the target on the island, your request has been granted. You have been reassigned to "Blackbird." According to her Watcher she is in strong physical and mental health. Your hunt will resume on September 21 at midnight. Await word from your Stager, who will provide information regarding the target's location.*

Your stomach tightens, your hands bloodless and cold. Ivan was your Stager, tracking you to and from different locations, reporting your whereabouts. You were Hilary's target, but when she was killed, her husband was reassigned to you—he *asked* to be reassigned to you. But who is the Watcher? The man with the black hat, the one Ivan reported to? How did the hunter find you the second time, when you were walking with Izzy that day? You think back to everyone you encountered on your walk, to the man giving the free stress test, and then you realize—that girl in front of the health-food store handed a coupon to Izzy. It was in Izzy's sweatshirt on your walk. It must be how they tracked you.

You pause when you hear a noise from downstairs. You look around, suddenly aware of all the windows in the bedroom. There's an open door right behind you, a bathroom to your left. You roll up the papers and tuck them into the back of your jeans. Then you reach for the knife.

CHAPTER THIRTY-SEVEN

YOU START DOWN the hallway when you hear a familiar voice. "What the hell?"

Izzy is standing at the top of the stairs. She glances around, looking into the master bedroom, at the overturned drawers and the clothes scattered on the floor. "This is what you had to do? This is what couldn't wait? You had to come rob these people?"

"Izzy, we have to get out of here," you say.

"Yeah, you bet we do. This is what you've been doing? Ransacking houses?"

She doesn't even finish the sentence when you hear it. The metal creak of the gate opening. You turn into the office, looking out over the driveway. His car—the same black Mercedes that followed you—pulls to a stop just beyond the front door. You turn to Izzy, grabbing her arm, pulling her toward the stairs.

"Just come with me," you say. "Don't say anything. Don't make any noise."

"What is it?" Her arm is tense beneath your grip. "What's wrong?"

You turn back, looking out the window, but the car is empty. There's the sound of the key in the lock. Then the door downstairs opens.

"He's here."

"You know these people?" Izzy whispers.

There's no time. You usher Izzy into the hall closet, pressing a finger to your lips. You close the door gently. You have barely made it a few steps before he appears at the bottom of the stairs. He lifts his pant leg, pulling a small pistol from a holster hidden at his calf. He doesn't aim it, though. He doesn't run up the stairs. He just smiles, as if he's been waiting for you all along.

"Did you miss me?" he asks.

He climbs the stairs slowly, coming toward you. You're aware of Izzy in the closet right behind you. You can't leave her there. You keep your body positioned between him and the closet door, knowing you'll have to lure him away.

"I remember what you did on the island," you say, conscious of the knife tucked at your hip. He's not close enough yet for it to be of any use. "You cut your chin. You were choking me. I remember you."

Goss shakes his head. "I've heard some of you were getting

your memories back. I've tried to look at it as incentive to kill quicker, before there are any complications."

"So do it, then," you say. "If you want me dead why wait even a second longer?"

"Because it's always the saddest part," he says. "Right at the end. Because all that time, that waiting . . . it's over. And there'll be satisfaction, of course, but the joy of it is in the build."

He reaches the top of the stairs, leaning casually on the banister, just a few feet from you. His gun is still in his hand, aimed just below your heart.

"So you remember the island, then? I'd tracked you for five days, right at the end. Everyone said you couldn't be taken but I knew I almost had you. It felt close. I'd found where you'd been staying with that boy, that den you'd made. I was always just a few hours behind you."

"The boy?"

Goss laughs. "You didn't bring him, did you? You used to work as a pair then. Cal thinks that's the only reason you survived."

He takes the next two steps. You inch backward, hiding your right side from him. You bring your hand to your hip, feeling for the end of the knife. "I survived again, here. Twice."

"It's harder to kill here, you know that. Too many chances for people to see. But on the island, it felt . . . unbridled.

There was total freedom. I tracked you to the north end. You were below, on those rocks, sleeping—that's where I found you. *Do I kill her while she's asleep? Or do I wait for her to see me, to know that fear, to really see it as it happens?* I fired at the rocks below to wake you. But it was a mistake. By the time I fired again you were already up, diving off the cliff."

He's closer now. His gun is still aimed at you. You could close the space in three steps. You're trying to gauge how fast you can strike, how effectively, when there's a thud inside the closet behind you. Goss's eyes flick to the door.

He doesn't hesitate. He raises the gun, firing once into the center of it. You hear Izzy's low, muffled yell, and something inside you breaks. You lunge, driving the knife into his side.

He jerks back, losing his balance, slipping down the staircase. One leg gives out, sending him skidding on his side. As the stairs curve he careens into the wall, hitting his head.

You open the closet. Izzy is slumped in the corner, pressing her hand to her side, her fingers covered in blood. There's a tiny hole in her sweatshirt, right beneath her ribs.

You tuck your shoulder under her arm, pulling her to stand. At the other end of the hall there's a narrow staircase. You move her toward it, listening to Goss below, his stunned murmurs as he picks himself back up. "You have to try to walk," you say. "I know it's hard, but try."

You urge her down the narrow flight, out a side foyer. You're in the back of the house now, the garden providing some cover. You move toward a gate below, which leads to the hillside.

You hear a door open somewhere behind you. He is up again; he is following you. You pick Izzy up, all one hundred pounds of her, and run as fast as you can, feeling the papers fall out of your back pocket. There's no time. You push through the metal gate and down the back of the hillside.

You hear Goss running around the side of the house, trying to figure out where you've gone. "We'll never make it," Izzy says.

She pulls up her shirt, studying the wound, pressing her fingers into it as if she's not sure it's real. You shake your head and keep moving, wishing it were you. It should have been you.

The house is on a hill and you find your way to a dirt path leading down. It's so steep you keep slipping. Along the back of his property there are eucalyptus trees, their trunks twisting up toward the sky. You can't hear him behind you. Has he gone the other way?

As soon as you're around the side of the fence, out of sight, you ease Izzy down. She leans back against the tree, her hand still pressing down on the wound.

Her hair sticks to her skin. Her face is twisted with worry, her breaths raspy. Watching her, you know that she could die here. She *will* die here if you don't do something.

"You'll be all right. He wants me," you say, "not you. I'm

going to get help. Keep pressing down on it. Don't move; stay awake."

You hold your hand over her hand, pushing onto the wound. A red stain spreads out beneath your fingers. The fabric is soaked through.

"I'm going to get help," you repeat. "I promise, Izzy."

She offers a weak nod before her eyes close.

You run, cutting up the steep hill as fast as you can. Every muscle in your legs burns, but you keep going, weaving through until you're on the road. You don't stop. You crane your head and he appears behind you, a hundred yards off. He is at the end of the driveway, waiting.

CHAPTER THIRTY-EIGHT

HE IS ABOUT to shoot when you take a hard left, cutting through a neighbor's yard. You hop a low stone fence, your sneakers sliding against the dirt path. You grab onto brush and vines, trying to stay up, but it's useless. You fall, slipping, skidding, your legs scraping against rock. As you slide farther down you catch the roots of a dead tree. You hold yourself there, looking back. Above you, the wall is empty. He hasn't followed you down.

You climb the rest of the way. Your hands grab branches and vines, clinging to dead roots, feet fitting into the dips and ledges in the rock. When you get to the street below it's empty. There's not a single car parked there. Every house is behind a huge gate, so far back you can't even see them.

You pull the phone Celia gave you from your pocket, grateful for it—for this gift, for her help. As soon as the operator answers you speak, the words coming together in a breathless stream. "My friend has been shot. She's at 2187 Glendower Avenue. She's behind the house, near the back of the yard. She's bleeding—she needs help now."

You can't wait for much of a response. When you're certain they've got the information you hang up and keep moving. Ben's house is several miles east, and you know you can outrun Goss once you're somewhere with more people, where he can't shoot without being seen. You just have to get to the boulevard below, two streets down.

You run, keeping along the edge of the street. You've gone for a few minutes, maybe more, when you hear him behind you. Glancing back, he's running up the edge of the road. He has a hat on now, sunglasses. You're cutting across, trying to avoid him, when he aims.

You sprint up the side of the pavement, unsure when a few seconds pass and he hasn't fired. Then you hear the engine behind you. You turn back. A red van has stopped at the edge of a driveway.

The side reads STARGAZER TOURS in block print. A man walks up and down an aisle of people with a microphone, pointing to a house over the gate. He mentions some action-movie star, then says something else that makes the people laugh. Behind him, Goss has stopped by another mailbox. His gun is now hidden. He walks slowly, methodically, toward you. The van doesn't move.

You know it's your chance. While the people are turned, studying the house, you run. You don't look back. You just keep going, until the street winds down to the boulevard below, a rush of traffic beside you.

———

When you return to Ben's house he's not there. You want to wait for him, to explain, but there's no time.

You sift through Ben's drawers, looking for checks, money—anything you can use. There are two credit cards that you pocket, enough to get you a cab ride or a ticket out of Los Angeles. You think of the photo, of the label *Los Angeles Target*. There are other targets in other cities, hunts going on around the country, maybe around the world. Where are those other targets now? Do any of them remember what happened to them, do any of them know what they're caught up in?

The game is elaborate, the network huge—you understand that now. Goss is just one hunter among many. You need to get out of here, you need to stay alive long enough to figure out your next move.

There are a few stray dollars in the bottom of the drawer. You take those, along with a glass jar of silver coins sitting next to the couch. As you tuck it under your arm you feel sick. You imagine Ben there, realizing they're gone, realizing that you took them.

You're nearly to the back door when you see his computer

on the kitchen table. The idea of not saying anything, of not saying good-bye . . . it's too much. You flip it open to write him a note.

You're searching the screen for a document to write in when you catch sight of it. A folder in the corner of his desktop labeled *AAE*.

AAE.

A&A Enterprises.

You open it and there are hundreds of documents inside. You click through to an image of you—the same one from Goss's house. You're staring into the camera. You already look half dead.

The room feels smaller, the walls rushing to meet you. It's so hard to breathe. You think of the file. *The Watcher.* Ben's known all along. He works for the people who are after you. The people trying to kill you. He is your Watcher.

You're not sure how long you've been sitting there when the lock turns. The door opens. Then Ben steps inside, all smiles.

"Hey, beautiful."

CHAPTER THIRTY-NINE

"IT WAS GOOD that I went," Ben says, dropping his keys on the entryway table. "She was upset I hadn't picked up the phone, upset about all the school stuff. I promised I was doing okay. I'm going to go back in three weeks when she's released. Until then . . . I'm yours."

He sets his hands down on your shoulders and his fingers work into your skin, kneading the muscles. But you are frozen beneath his touch. You're only aware of how close his hands are to your neck and the distance between the kitchen table and the door.

"What's wrong?" He leans down, staring into your face. "It's going to be okay, I promise. We can go now, I just need another minute or two."

You stand, slipping out from underneath him. "It's just a lot to process," you say. "That's all. Let me just get my bag from the pool house."

You don't look at him as you go. You can't. Instead you start for the door, almost out of the kitchen, almost into the hall.

"What's this about?" he asks, picking up the glass jar of coins from underneath the table. "Were you taking this? What's going on?"

You pause in the doorway, debating whether you should try to explain. He's studying your face. Then, as if it has just registered, he looks down at the computer on the table, then back at you. He flips it open. Your picture is still there, still open on the desktop. It stares up at him.

You go for the back door but he is already coming after you. "It's not what you think," he says. "Please, you just have to listen."

You get out the door but he jams his hand against the frame, stopping it from shutting. You push back, crushing his fingers. You hit the door again, wincing each time it lands, each time you hear his skin and bone catch beneath the frame. But then, finally, he lets go. You hop the fence into another yard. You keep running, weaving through a wooden area, not stopping until you are back on the street.

CHAPTER FORTY

AS SOON AS she steps through the gate, she begins her routine. She scans the front gardens, checking to see how much the plumeria have grown in her absence. She'll have to cut the branches back from the window. They replaced the grass in the front with gravel the year before so she no longer has to worry about the overgrowth when they're not there. Leaves are gathered around the front entrance, but otherwise it looks fine. No one has tried to break in.

She has begged her husband to get someone to watch over the property while they're in the States, but Michael always refuses. *It's impossible to get here by boat. It's a private island; what's the point?* He won't listen to her when she argues about what happened three years before, how they found the lock on the front gate broken, a knife lying just outside the door. He'd been game hunting on the south of the island with friends.

He hadn't noticed anything suspicious, had pointed out it was near impossible for someone to approach the house from the north shore. The property was gated, sitting atop a rock cliff. But she hasn't forgotten about it. She still wonders if it could have been one of the men he was with.

There were other things, too. . . .

That tree she'd seen on a walk one morning last year, the trunk smeared with blood. The forest smelled different to her, a strange, sickening stench drifting in when the wind changed directions. She used to spend all her time in the woods beyond the fence, hiking the stone paths the previous owners had carved out, cutting the black orchids that grew along it. She hardly goes out there at all anymore.

She turns the key in the lock, knowing it'll be another two days before Michael returns from his hunting trip on the south side of the island. She left a message on the machine at the house but there's no way to reach him when he's in the woods, no real way to tell him she's arrived early.

When she pushes the door open, the alarm sounds. She goes to the keypad, punching in the code to silence it, then turns to the wall of windows that overlooks the ocean. The view always surprises her, even more when she's been gone for several months. It's nothing but water in every direction. She always arranges for the plane to drop her in the field an hour before sunset, so that by the time she gets to the house the sky is a bright pink, the sun a yellow disk slipping behind the western cliff face.

The house is completely silent. She goes to the glass wall in the living room, looking out. Far below, the tide is coming in, the waves rushing over the sand, colliding into the rocks. She stares over the horizon, turning back toward the western sky, and that's when she sees it.

There's writing on the side of one of the rocks. It's ten feet up from where the water hits. Someone would've had to scale the cliff face to get to it, balancing on one of the narrow ledges in the stone. The writing is brownish-red, though she can't quite make out the letters from so high up.

She goes to the desk in the corner of the living room, pulling her husband's binoculars from the top drawer, and looks out through the lenses. She turns the dial at the top to bring the writing into focus.

Her hands shake as she reads it, processing the messy scrawl. Out on the cliff below is a dark red stain. Just four letters.

HELP.

Michael. It has to be. She scans the house, looking for something, anything, to bring with her. The nearest hospital is an hour's flight away. Is he still alive? How long ago did he write that? He must've slipped on the trail; he must be trapped there, on the cliff ledge.

She runs out of the front gate, hurrying down the path, the thin branches scraping at her legs. It's not more than ten minutes to the cliffs. She weaves through the trees, blocking her face with her hand. She had told him to bring the flares with him when he hunts, had suggested radios or something for him to communicate with the others. Why hadn't he agreed to it? Why was he so stubborn, so determined for the hunts to be authentic, real?

There's a noise behind her. Something moves in the forest, darting through the trees. She turns, watching. With the sun going down they are only shadows at first, two of them cutting out on either side, circling her. Then she sees one man start over a log, approaching her from the front. He has the hunting rifle out. He looks directly at her, meeting her gaze, as he fires once into the center of her chest.

She falls back, the thick awning of leaves visible overhead. For only a few moments she's still conscious, taking in the small patch of pink sky, then Michael's face above hers. "What happened? What did you do?" she asks.

Michael turns to the other man, his voice rising in panic. "It wasn't her; it wasn't the girl. You just killed my wife."

CHAPTER FORTY-ONE

THE HOSPITAL LOBBY is nearly empty. A light buzzes over-head. An older woman with a cane sits on a cushioned chair, her head hanging to one side, mouth open in sleep. In an office down the hall, someone is listening to a love song.

You keep your head down. You were able to withdraw cash off Ben's credit cards and you are wearing a new flow-ered dress that Izzy would hate. You have new glasses and your hair is pulled into a tight bun, the scar covered with a thin scarf. The nurse is reading a book on her desk, a fat paperback, and you walk past, hoping she doesn't see. You're several steps down the hall when she stops you.

"Excuse me? Where do you think you're going?" She stands, hands on hips. She's heavyset, nearly a foot taller than you, her curves filling out her pink scrubs.

"I'm looking for a girl who was shot," you say. "She came in today."

The woman shakes her head. "I don't care who you're looking for. It's nearly ten o'clock."

"Please," you say. "I called. No one would tell me anything. I just need to know if she's okay."

You've tried to push the thought away, but you can't—it keeps coming back, keeps flooding in every time you think of leaving. It's possible they got to Izzy first. If she was discovered there, behind Goss's house, they would've gotten rid of her body. The ambulance would've shown up and found only a dry patch of dirt.

"Please—I just need to know."

She holds up one finger, silencing you. Then she writes down something on a piece of paper. She folds it, then holds it up. "Now I have the room number right here. But I'm going to need you to tell me her name. No one seems to know who this girl is."

"So she's okay?"

"For now."

"And if I give you her name, will you let me see her?"

"I'll give you ten minutes before I call the police. I don't know what happened to that girl, but they've already been here twice today trying to figure it out. I have a feeling they'd be interested in talking to you."

"Izzy Clark," you say. You root around your bag, feeling

for the letter you wrote. You dropped the file from Goss's house in the rush to get out, but you've written out everything that happened, naming A&A Enterprises, describing the secret compartment in the top of the closet. You've written everything they need to know.

The woman slips you the folded note. You set the envelope on the counter. You put *Celia Alvarez, LAPD* on the front, hoping that it will eventually make its way to her. "This is for them, when they get here."

Then you set off down the hall, unfolding the note. *701* is written, the numbers underlined twice. You walk along the edge of the wall, where the surveillance cameras don't have as good an angle on you. Then you turn, climbing the stairs to avoid being seen.

When you get to Izzy's room a nurse is there and you have to wait in the hall, just inside a linen closet, until she leaves. You can feel the minutes ticking away. You listen to the sounds of footsteps on the tile floor, making sure the hall is quiet before going back in.

Izzy is in bed. There are tubes everywhere. They snake around her, twisting up into a bag of fluid, hanging down beneath the metal bedframe. Her eyes are taped shut. Her skin is a dull gray color and it takes looking at the monitor, watching her pulse rise and fall, to be certain she's alive.

You go to her, touching the top of her hand. Her skin feels papery and strange. The IV is stuck in, the blood sticky and wet beneath the clear tape. You can't tell if she knows you're there. You just talk, leaning down so she can hear.

"Mims should be here soon," you say. "I'm so sorry you've been alone. I'm sorry about everything."

You sit there, listening to each of her breaths. You can almost see Goss, the way he looked this afternoon when he shot her. You can picture him and Hilary in the photo. You remember his face more clearly than ever before.

The boy's voice comes back: *We're not murderers*. Somehow this time, you don't believe him. All you can think of is Izzy, how sick and weak she looks now, like someone has drained the life out of her. You squeeze her hand once more before you go.

CHAPTER FORTY-TWO

UNION STATION IS bustling with rush-hour foot traffic. Swarms of people push through the main hall. A woman with a massive suitcase bumps you from behind. Another person swerves around you, mumbling something that could be directed at you, but maybe not. You don't look up. You keep walking, moving toward one of the side lounges, where it's less crowded. There are only fifteen minutes until the train leaves, but you know that doesn't mean anything. That's enough time to be seen.

You check the train on the sign above, the letters and numbers flipping in place, shifting and rearranging as some arrive and depart. CHICAGO, IL. 11:15 P.M. ON TIME. In two days you'll be far away from Los Angeles, in a new city, disappearing into the mass of people there. You want to believe they won't find you, that they can't. But it might be just a matter of time.

What did Ben know? What has he told them? You've tried to go through the past week, dissecting what you said to him, trying to figure out how you had missed it. Every moment seems false. How many times had he said that you were safe in that house? What did he know that you didn't? Had it been the truth, or was it inevitable that they would've come for you there? Would he have let them? What was the point of keeping you alive? Was running away part of their plan—or was it something different, was it part of his?

A few people look up as you pass and you can't tell if they're looking at you or at the board above. You cover your face with your hand, pretending to fix your hair. *Fifteen minutes,* you remind yourself. Just fifteen minutes more. Then you'll be on the train, moving away from here.

All of the lounges are off the main corridor. You pass the first one, which has just a few empty seats. You pass the second, then the third, only stopping when you find the one that's quietest, the least crowded. The chairs all face the wall. There are only three other people there. Two men absorbed in their phones, and a woman who has fallen asleep, her head propped up on her purse.

You grab a seat as far from them as possible, your back to the crowds that pass. It's been an hour since you left the hospital. You've followed the time, thinking about the police officers opening the envelope, calling Izzy's grandmother,

Mims arriving at the hospital. By now she should be there with her. By now they should have read your letter. They should be at Goss's house, questioning him, looking for the compartment in his closet . . . if he hasn't found a way to conceal it.

"The train to Chicago will begin boarding in five minutes," an announcement says. A few people get up, some dragging bags behind them.

Across the aisle you notice a homeless guy curled up, sleeping beneath three of the seats. One of the men tucks away his phone and stands, rolling a small bag behind him. But the aisle is narrow and there isn't enough room to pass.

"What are you doing under there? You're blocking the path!" The man leans down and picks up his bag, mumbling something under his breath.

The guy pushes out, grabbing a pack from the floor beside him. He brushes himself off and stands. He plucks a ticket from his pocket. Then he turns his face up, trying to catch sight of the board. His eyes meet yours, and you are suddenly the only two people there. They're *his* eyes—brown, liquid, and warm. His cheeks, his lips, which you've kissed a hundred times before, the top one dipping in a deep V. The two freckles on his right cheek. His hair is longer, covering his brows, but you'd know him anywhere.

The bottom of his shirt is ripped. His pants are covered with dirt. You look down at his right wrist and you can see it, peeking out behind a plastic watch. The square has its own number, its own symbol, though you can't quite decipher what it is.

You watch him watching you, taking in your clothes, the sleek bun, the scarf around your neck. You pull back the leather wristband, showing him the tender skin on the inside of your wrist. You hold your hand so no one else can see.

"You," he finally says. "It's you."

Then he smiles. You can barely breathe you feel so much for this person, this stranger, this boy from your dreams.

"You're here," you say as he comes toward you. "You're real."

ACKNOWLEDGMENTS

THIS BOOK WOULDN'T be possible without the support and care of several people. First and foremost, hugs and thank-yous to everyone at Alloy Entertainment. To Les Morgenstein, for pushing the first chapters to another draft, which really made the voice sing. To Josh Bank, for all his love and enthusiasm for this project, and for those supportive tweets (you are the Walrus, goo goo goo joob). To Sara Shandler, for all her meticulous line edits, for seeing the things we couldn't, and for her smarts and patience in an eleventh-hour revision. And to Joelle Hobeika, editor and friend, for her continual faith, support, and all-around awesomeness. Thank you for talking me through said eleventh-hour revision, assuring me the book would be better, that I was almost there, and that it would be worth it (it was).

To my editor at HarperCollins, Sarah Landis, for her patience and support while this book grew from those first few chapters into what it is now. You've loved it from page one and were the first to say: YES! Second person works! That meant so much. Gratitude to Kristin Marang, for helping me with all things digital. To Heather Schroder, agent and confidante, for her good work and guidance.

I'm grateful for the close friends who read the very first pages of this book, letting me know there was something there . . . even if I wasn't quite sure what it was yet. Love and thanks to Lauren Kate Morphew, Aaron Kandell, and Allison Yarrow. To Amy Plum and Natalie Parker, who took time and care when they were busy with their own revisions to read mine. Special thanks to the inimitable Josie Angelini, superhero to YA novels everywhere, for the notes that inspired this last draft.

I'm lucky to have a wide network of friends and family who keep me sane and grounded when life is anything but. To the authors I've toured and traveled with—Veronica Rossi, Tahereh Mafi, and Cynthia Hand—I'm grateful to count you as friends. Much love and thanks to: Lanie Davis, Anna Zupon, Jess Dickstein, Katie Sise, Jackie Fechtmann, Ally Paul, Ali Mountford, Amy Hand, Dana Nichomoff, Laurie Porter, Connie Hsiao, Deb Gross, Melva Graham, Talia Reyes, Priya Ollapally, Jordan Kandell, Jon Fletcher, and Corynne Cirilli. As always, love to my family on the

East Coast for reading every book and cheering me on. To my brother, Kevin, medical consultant, friend, publicist: This one is for you. And to my parents, Tom and Elaine, for boundless love and support. I. A. E. I. A. B. O. Y.